Embark on a metaphysical journey, transcending reality's lines to unveil mysteries in the spaces in between.

SKIPPING THE LINES OF REALITY

A LEAP BEYOND THE NORM

KOUSUMI CHAUDHURI

BlueRoseONE.com
Stories Matter
NewDelhi • London

BLUEROSE PUBLISHERS
India | U.K.

BlueRose ONE
Stories Matter
NewDelhi • London

For permissions requests or inquiries regarding this publication, please contact:

BLUEROSE PUBLISHERS
www.BlueRoseONE.com
info@bluerosepublishers.com
+91 8882 898 898
+4407342408967

ISBN: 978-93-5989-280-1

Cover Design: Muskan Sachdeva
Typesetting: Pooja Sharma

First Edition: April 2024

Thanks to BlueRose and my friends who have encouraged me to write this book.

The main plot:

The reason that lets you smile

The accompany that let every hardship turn out fine

The bond that complements your flaws that you find

I think that's the love that you keep deep in your mind.

The day ended well for her... got a new look just like shedding a worn tired torn skin loaded with tons of dumped desires further getting into a newer version ignoring the parental and societal judgments and restrictions.... After enjoying a sumptuous homemade dinner and grilling chickens she came back to the cocoon she created, and said to herself 'Ah! This day needs to end. I've had enough of the day' and just laid on her bed...just to escape the racing competing and ruthless harsh talker world which the entire world generalized as a room.

With the music softly creating a world of delusion, a sudden strike of a bunch of golden memories and moments, brought a lovable smile to her consumed face. Soothing herself with the musical magic, she pulled herself up to complete her one last work of watering her little garden and opening the window to create a passage of fresh cool air to breathe in the room. Tickling the glass pots she talked to the plants with an expression of joy, 'Well, someone has grown today!' cleaning the little dust off the leaves of the money plants, she lit the fairy lights, which were rounded over the side corner of the desk casting a soft, ethereal glow. The click of the most loveable tracks lightened the mood of the room, she dragged the bin bag and crawled over to it, as the bin bag got the best comfort spot the reminiscence of them flashed right before her eyes and left a drop of tear on their way back....

Each verse of the playlist gave her goosebumps reminding the tensions of each lovable moment that once she shared and thought to be HER forever.

Adveka, the name that had been ruling the college campus; always remained in the limelight of every field; now enjoyed her low-key life just in survival mode to bring a ray of hope to encourage her to breathe. She had a lovely dream of enjoying a corporate house in the middle of the city one among the skyscrapers and being surrounded by well-tailored suits and ties; just to ensure the demands of her domineering parents she had to leave all those behind and opt for the corporate landscape she had hated for long.

Clutching the pillows tightly to her chest, she stifled the teary thoughts that threatened to overwhelm her. With determination, she closed her eyes, allowing the comforting luminescence of the fairy lights to soothe her troubled mind. As the weight of the upcoming morning hustle loomed, she embraced the tranquility, letting sleep sweep her into its embrace, offering a reprieve from the demands of the waking world.

Adveka, the resilient soul molded by the crucible of a challenging past, found herself navigating the labyrinth of the corporate world. Behind the polished exterior of her tailored suits and amidst the skyscrapers, she bore the scars of a toxic upbringing and a tumultuous college life. Colleagues admired her dedication, oblivious to the shadows that lingered in her past.

Her days were a delicate dance, a ballet of financial jargon and strategic maneuvers. Adveka, once the luminary of her college, had transformed into a quiet force within the corporate landscape. She had traded the spotlight for the shadows, choosing survival over the chaos of her past.

In her corner office, surrounded by the city's heartbeat, Adveka's dreams seemed within reach. Yet, the pressure of corporate expectations mirrored the demands of her domineering parents. Each day, she donned her armor of resilience, battling not only for professional success but also for a semblance of control over her life.

The boardroom became her battlefield, and the spreadsheets her allies. Colleagues marveled at her leadership, unaware of the silent battles she fought within. Adveka's strength wasn't just a product of corporate prowess; it was a testament to the triumph of spirit over adversity.

Within the hallowed halls of the corporate landscape where Adveka strove for success, a subtler battle raged—office politics and jealousy. Her dedication and hard work, once commendable, stirred envy in the hearts of some colleagues who viewed her ascent with a mix of admiration and resentment.

As Adveka meticulously climbed the professional ladder, her peers, hungry for recognition, became entangled in the intricate web of office politics. Whispers of jealousy followed her like shadows, echoing in the hallways and boardrooms. Adveka's resilience and exceptional work ethic made her a target for those who sought to undermine her success.

Colleagues, instead of celebrating her achievements, questioned her methods and speculated about hidden alliances. Adveka's ability to effortlessly navigate challenges and garner praise from superiors fueled the flames of resentment among those who struggled to match her pace.

The office grapevine buzzed with gossip, and subtle acts of sabotage attempted to chip away at Adveka's hard-earned reputation. Yet, she remained focused, channeling the negativity into fuel for her determination. The jealous whispers only strengthened her resolve to succeed on her terms.

Adveka's dedication became both a source of admiration and a thorn in the side of those who aimed to undermine her. The more she excelled, the louder the whispers of jealousy grew. Despite the politics swirling around her, Adveka continued to lead with integrity, refusing to compromise her values for the sake of fleeting recognition.

Amid office politics and envy, Adveka's journey became a testament to not only her professional prowess but also her ability to navigate the treacherous waters of corporate dynamics. The challenges she faced fueled her determination, transforming the workplace into a battleground where resilience and authenticity triumphed over jealousy and intrigue.

As her journey unfolded, Adveka's past whispered its echoes. Late nights were haunted by memories of a time when her name echoed through college corridors, a beacon of leadership and camaraderie. Now, it was whispered in hushed tones, a testament to the sacrifices made for survival. The one who used to be the talk of the rooms and mouths, now used to talk to herself holding up to herself just to push her patience over a little more to extend the extent... at times she felt like it was not she who had a burning spirit in the eyes, she had started to avoid looking over mirrors as the days and the present had pushed her to the cliff of her self-esteem where her self-respect started to question her.

In the quiet moments between deadlines, Adveka stared out of her office window, her gaze reaching beyond the concrete jungle. The city's lights mirrored the fairy lights she once switched on to escape the harsh reality. Yet, in the quietude of those moments, a glimmer of hope emerged. The dreams of a corporate house amid skyscrapers, once a compromise, now became a beacon of possibility.

Adveka, the phoenix of her own story, rose from the ashes of her past, not just surviving but thriving in a world that had once seemed insurmountable. The corporate journey, though laden with challenges, became a canvas for her resilience, a testament to the indomitable spirit that refused to be extinguished.

In the heart of Adveka's corporate cocoon, a new chapter unfolded with the arrival of Raivat, a colleague two years her senior in both age and corporate experience. His presence added a new layer to the intricacies of the office landscape. Adveka, in the shadows of her past, found herself drawn to the enigma that was Raivat. The boardroom discussions became a symphony of their unspoken connection, each project a canvas where their professional collaboration danced on the edge of something more. Adveka couldn't deny the flutter in her heart, the subtle blush that colored her cheeks when Raivat entered the room. As she navigated the corporate battlefield, the clandestine glances and stolen smiles hinted at a secret crush blooming amidst the spreadsheets and deadlines. The fairy lights that once shone for solace now held the soft glow of shared moments, weaving a tale of emotions as complex as the office politics that surrounded them.

Contents

Chapter 1

The Thread of Fate

In the sprawling metropolis where the city's heartbeat echoed through towering skyscrapers, two individuals, Adveka and Raivat, emerged from different worlds, each carrying their unique tales of triumph and struggle.

Adveka, a prodigy with a brilliant mind, was born into a world of contrasts. Raised in the shadows of her narcissistic parents, who valued success over empathy, she found solace in the realm of numbers. The world of finance became her refuge, a place where logic and strategy provided the stability and order lacking in her tumultuous family life.

Adveka's journey was one of resilience. She navigated the challenges of her upbringing with determination, channeling the pain into a relentless pursuit of excellence. Her rise in the financial world was meteoric, breaking through gender and societal barriers to become one of the youngest and most successful bankers at the prestigious firm.

Raivat, on the other hand, hailed from a background where the struggle was not just financial but also rooted in the pursuit of dreams. Growing up in a modest neighborhood, he faced adversity with a charming smile and an insatiable thirst for knowledge. Finance, for Raivat, was not merely a career path but a ladder to climb, a means to elevate himself beyond the limitations of his humble beginnings.

The paths of Adveka and Raivat converged at the doors of the same banking firm, where ambition and intellect were the currency that mattered most. They collided in the whirlwind of numbers, charts, and late-night meetings, their shared passion creating a synergy that was palpable to those around them.

The invisible red thread of destiny began to weave itself, connecting these two individuals who, despite their different backgrounds, found common ground in the world of finance. Their collaboration on projects became a harmonious dance of intellect, each complementing the strengths and weaknesses of the other.

As they conquered professional challenges together, an unspoken understanding blossomed between them, transcending the boundaries of the corporate world. Adveka's brilliant mind found a partner in Raivat's charm, creating a dynamic duo that seemed destined for success.

Yet, amidst the triumphs of their professional lives, a silent tension lingered. Adveka's heart, hardened by the scars of her past, hesitated to unveil the emotions bubbling beneath the surface. The red thread of destiny, though subtly present, remained unseen, waiting to reveal its true nature as the story of Adveka and Raivat unfolded.

As Adveka and Raivat navigated the intricate world of finance together, their professional camaraderie became intertwined with subtle moments of connection that sparked a flame in Adveka's heart. The office, once a domain governed by numbers and strategies, now bore witness to the unspoken language of glances and shared moments.

A Shared Smile Across the Room:

In a bustling office day, there was a moment when Adveka looked up from her desk, - expecting to seek a little attention -found Raivat engrossed in a report across the room. She didn't expect to get him around her eyes as it was beyond Raivat's scheduled time to be there. As if searching for the same, Raivat turned around his head with a sharp look and a side eye, their eyes met, and in that fleeting second, a shared smile passed between them. It was a simple exchange, but in that moment, the invisible threads of fate stirred, weaving a narrative that went beyond the confines of the workplace.

For Adveka, whose heart still carried the scars of a traumatic and toxic past, the exchange of smiles became a balm to wounds she thought were irreparable. The warmth in Raivat's gaze became a beacon of hope, igniting a flicker of romance in the burnt-out, shattered chambers of her heart.

The Dance of Eyes During Late-Night Brainstorming:

Late-night brainstorming sessions became a canvas for a different kind of collaboration. As Adveka and Raivat delved into complex financial models, their eyes engaged in a silent dance of understanding. There was an unspoken connection, an exchange of ideas that transcended the verbal, leaving Adveka with a sense of fulfillment she had never known before. When Raivat used to find Adveka dozing off the desk in the middle of tiresome nights building models for the projects. Raivat gently nudges Adveka awake from her post-brainstorming slumber, he smirks playfully and says, "Did it hurt, Adveka? Because you must be tired from falling for this project, and I thought I should be the one to catch you before you hit the burnout." With a charming smile, he presents a steaming cup of coffee, the aroma filling the room. "Coffee for the dreamer, to fuel those brilliant ideas. Let's conquer this project together, one caffeine kick at a time."

In the romantic interplay of their glances, Adveka found solace. The traumatic echoes of her past began to fade as the fire kindled in her heart, fueled by the gentle warmth of Raivat's gaze. His eyes, mirrors of understanding, reflected a world where professional collaboration seamlessly intertwined with the delicate dance of burgeoning emotions.

A Tender Touch During a Celebration:

The project turned out to be the biggest success to date and had been a benchmark in Adveka and Raivat's careers.

Amidst the celebration of successful project completion, Adveka and Raivat found themselves in a moment of shared triumph. As congratulations echoed through the office, Raivat, caught up in the joy of the moment, placed a congratulatory hand on Adveka's shoulder. It was a gesture both tender and spontaneous, sending ripples through the invisible threads of fate that bound them together.

For Adveka, the touch became a poignant reminder that not all connections were meant to be toxic. The tenderness in that moment spoke volumes, igniting a spark of romantic possibility in her heart. The fire that had long been extinguished by the harsh winds of her past traumas now flickered back to life, fueled by the genuine connection she shared with Raivat.

The Unspoken Language of Glances:

During meetings and discussions, there were stolen glances that spoke volumes. Raivat's eyes held a depth of understanding that transcended the professional realm, and Adveka, haunted by the scars of her toxic past, found refuge in those stolen moments.

During the joyous celebration of Adveka and Raivat's triumphant project success, Adveka couldn't help but be captivated by the alluring sharpness in Raivat's eyes. As the room reverberated with applause and cheers, she realized, with a romantic twinge in her heart, that for the first time, she had peered into someone's eyes and discovered features that held not a hint of domineering intention. In those blissful moments of shared accomplishment, she found herself entangled in Raivat's gaze, a connection that whispered of unspoken emotions and a budding romance beyond the confines of the corporate triumph.

The romantic dance of their glances became a sanctuary for Adveka, a reminder that love could be gentle, understanding, and free from the toxic bonds that had defined her past. Each exchanged look kindled a fire within her, a flame of hope that burned away the shadows of her traumatic history.

In the office crush that blossomed between Adveka and Raivat, the romantic moments woven into their professional tapestry became the antidote to the poison of Adveka's past. The flames of connection, ignited by shared glances and tender touches, offered a promise of healing and a chance at love untainted by the scars of toxic relationships.

In the world of finance, where numbers held sway, Adveka and Raivat found a sanctuary in their shared moments, building a connection that transcended the boundaries of professionalism. Amidst the hustle and bustle of the office, their story unfolded like a romanticized old-school tale, complete with stolen glances and timeless gestures.

A Shared Umbrella in the Rain:

On a rainy afternoon, when the city outside their office windows was veiled in a soft drizzle, Adveka and Raivat found themselves leaving the building at the same time. In an old-school twist, Raivat gallantly offered Adveka his umbrella. As they strolled through the rain-soaked streets, their laughter echoed like a melody, creating a timeless scene that spoke of chivalry and shared joy.

The romantic gesture of sharing an umbrella became a cherished memory for Adveka. The simple act of kindness from Raivat not only shielded them from the rain but also became a symbol of the gentle care he extended beyond the confines of their professional world.

A Handwritten Note of Encouragement:

In the age of digital communication, Raivat's choice to pen down a handwritten note for Adveka stood out as a gesture from a bygone era. The note, filled with words of encouragement and appreciation for Adveka's dedication, carried a warmth that transcended the pixels of modern messages. Raivat used to walk by the desk just in a question utters 'Hmm?' Her pointing to the date pasted over the edge of the monitor in a turned sticky note 'I'll be dead if this is not done by tomorrow!!' His eyes sparkled with genuine admiration as he pinned a note stating 'trust in your unique spark.' Adveka blushed and kept her over the note as if she tried to soak the energy and get boosted.

Adveka cherished the handwritten note as a romantic relic in the digital age. The personal touch in Raivat's words spoke directly to her heart, evoking a sense of connection that went beyond the typed messages exchanged in the corporate world.

A Shared Favorite Coffee Spot:

In the quaint coffee shop around the corner from their office, Adveka and Raivat discovered a shared love for old-school charm. Their impromptu coffee breaks became moments of respite from the demands of their roles, as they sipped on steaming cups of coffee and exchanged stories in an ambiance reminiscent of classic romance.

The coffee shop, with its vintage decor and the aroma of freshly ground beans, became a backdrop for their burgeoning connection. Adveka found herself drawn to the timeless atmosphere, where every shared cup seemed to deepen the threads of their connection.

A Dance at the Office Party:

In the glitz and glamour of an office party, Adveka and Raivat found themselves on the dance floor, swaying to the rhythm of a classic tune. The old-school charm of the moment transported them to an era where the dance floor was a canvas for unspoken emotions and the music a conduit for shared desires. The coincidently color-twined individuals enjoyed being dancing buddies. At moments when their steps brought them closer, their breathe skipped one heartbeat leading to the other one's racing....

As they moved together in a graceful dance, the romanticized ambiance of the party mirrored the growing intimacy between Adveka and Raivat. The unspoken connection that had woven itself through stolen glances and shared moments now found expression in the timeless language of dance.

A Gentle Touch During a Team Celebration:

During a team celebration, as they toasted to a successful project, Raivat's hand found Adveka's in a gentle clasp.

The touch, more intimate than a handshake yet innocent enough for a professional setting, sent ripples through the room. It was an old-school gesture that spoke of connection, understanding, and the promise of something more.

For Adveka, the gentle touch became a tender affirmation of the emotions she had been harboring. The romanticized interaction resonated with a simplicity that harked back to a time when connections were built on subtlety and genuine gestures.

In the romanticized old-school interactions between Adveka and Raivat, the office crush transformed into a timeless narrative. Stolen glances, handwritten notes, shared moments at a classic coffee shop, a dance at the office party, and a gentle touch during a celebration became the building blocks of a love story that echoed the charm of a bygone era.

Adveka and Raivat's connection, while enriched by old-school romance, also embraced the modern era, drawing inspiration from web series and internet sketches that defined the years 2018-2020. Their story unfolded in a blend of classic charm and contemporary moments.

A Shared Playlist and Podcasts:

In the digital age, Adveka and Raivat discovered a shared appreciation for music and podcasts. They exchanged playlists that spoke volumes about their personalities, discovering new songs and hidden gems. In a scene reminiscent of a modern romantic comedy, they discussed their favorite podcasts during lunch breaks, connecting over the digital waves that carried the voices of their favorite hosts.

The shared playlist became a virtual mixtape, a reflection of their evolving connection in the language of music. As they explored the digital realm of podcasts together, their bond deepened, creating a contemporary thread within the fabric of their romance.

Virtual Movie Nights:

Inspired by the trend of virtual movie nights that gained popularity during the years 2018-2020, Adveka and Raivat found a way to bridge the physical distance when work demands kept them apart. Through online streaming platforms and synchronized viewing, they shared the experience of watching the latest movies and binge-worthy series, turning mundane evenings into cinematic adventures.

In the glow of their respective screens, Adveka and Raivat explored a new dimension of connection. The shared commentary and laughter over video calls became a modern twist to their budding romance, mirroring the changing dynamics of relationships in the digital age.

Office Messaging Apps and Memes:

Navigating the nuances of office life in the modern era, Adveka and Raivat found a playful outlet for their conversations through office messaging apps. Memes, GIFs, and witty messages became the language through which they expressed camaraderie and shared the lighter moments of their workdays.

The exchange of humorous content from the internet sketches of the time became a modern-day love letter. The shared laughter over memes, a commentary on the quirks of office culture, and the inside jokes they developed added a layer of contemporary charm to their relationship.

Virtual Team Building and Online Challenges:

As the corporate world embraced virtual team-building activities, Adveka and Raivat found themselves collaborating on online challenges and activities. Whether it was participating in virtual escape rooms or joining team-building webinars, they navigated the digital landscape together, finding new ways to connect beyond the constraints of their physical office space.

The shared experience of virtual team building became a metaphor for their evolving connection. Through online challenges and collaborative endeavors, they discovered the strengths and intricacies of each other's personalities, weaving a narrative that mirrored the collaborative spirit of internet sketches prevalent during that period.

In the fusion of classic and modern moments, inspired by both old-school romance and the internet culture of the time, Adveka and Raivat's office crush unfolded as a tapestry woven with threads from different eras. The blend of timeless gestures and contemporary interactions created a narrative that resonated with the complexities and beauty of love in the digital age.

Amidst the conversation that echoed with the echoes of their shared history, there were moments of painful silence. The unspoken words hung heavy in the air, a testament to the emotions that dared not surface. In those silent intervals, the red thread of destiny seemed to tighten its grip, weaving a narrative of unfulfilled longing and unspoken confessions.

As the conversation unfolded, the unspoken pain of Adveka became increasingly evident. The cityscape, which had once witnessed their shared triumphs, now bore witness to the heartbreaking unraveling of the connection that had defined their professional journey.

In the aftermath of this emotionally charged encounter, Adveka, with tear-stained eyes, made a silent decision to part ways. The tapestry that once held the promise of connection now bore the stains of unspoken confessions and unfulfilled desires. With each step away from Raivat, she left behind the echoes of a love never expressed and the haunting memories of a bond that had both sustained and shattered her.

The city, unmoved by the personal tragedies within its midst, witnessed the quiet departure of a heartbroken Adveka. The threads of fate, now entangled with the painful residue of unfulfilled love, continued to weave a narrative of separation and introspection. As Adveka moved away, the threads that once bound them together unraveled further, leaving behind a trail of heartache and unspoken emotions.

The revelation of Raivat's existing relationship shattered Adveka's world, leaving behind a mosaic of emotions that demanded her attention. The pain was palpable, and she found herself at a crossroads, faced with the daunting task of picking up the shattered pieces of her heart.

Breaking Away from Euphoria:

Adveka, once fueled by the euphoria of professional success and the camaraderie with Raivat, now found herself in a starkly different reality. The vibrant hues of her achievements dulled, and the once-invigorating office environment became a haunting reminder of a bond that was never reciprocated. The invisible red thread that had bound them together now seemed more like a chain, restraining her from emotional liberation.

In a bold move that mirrored the strength she had cultivated over the years, Adveka opted for a career switch. The decision was not merely a change of job; it was a conscious effort to distance herself from the echoes of her unrequited feelings. She needed a clean break, a new canvas upon which to paint the next chapter of her life.

Picking Up Broken Pieces:

The first days in her new professional realm were a mix of vulnerability and determination. Adveka faced the challenge of adapting to a different industry, a world where she was no longer the seasoned expert but a novice eager to learn. The pain of unfulfilled emotions lingered, but amidst the chaos, she discovered a reservoir of inner strength.

The switch became a metaphorical shedding of old skin. Adveka embraced the discomfort of the unfamiliar, channeling the energy from her painful past into a driving force for self-discovery. The red thread of destiny, though seemingly severed, continued to guide her, nudging her towards a path of resilience and personal growth.

Moving Away from Raivat's Reflections:

The decision to change careers was not just a professional pivot but a deliberate strategy to distance herself from the constant reminders of Raivat. Every corridor, every meeting room, and every fleeting glance seemed to hold reflections of a past that stung. Adveka needed space - a blank canvas where she could redefine herself beyond the shadows of unrequited love.

In her new role, Adveka immersed herself in challenges, determined to prove her capabilities in a fresh environment. The red thread of destiny, now a subtle guide rather than a binding force, urged her to forge a destiny free from the emotional entanglements that had once defined her existence.

As Adveka navigated the painful start of her new journey, she began to realize the transformative power of her choices. The invisible threads of karma and fate were at play, weaving a narrative of resilience, self-discovery, and the inevitable convergence of paths that awaited her and Raivat in the chapters yet to unfold.

As Adveka stumbled through the agonizing commencement of her new journey, the weight of her heartbreak bore down on her fragile shoulders. In the merciless echoes of her unreciprocated emotions, she found herself painfully aware of the profound impact her choices were having on the tapestry of her existence. The invisible threads of karma and fate seemed less like benevolent guides and more like merciless puppeteers, orchestrating a tragic narrative of victimhood.

Each step she took in her unfamiliar professional realm felt like a reluctant surrender to a destiny that mocked her vulnerability. The red thread, once a hopeful promise of connection, now seemed like an unforgiving noose tightening around her, a relentless reminder of love unreturned. Adveka, unwittingly cast as the victim in this cruel play, grappled with the realization that her choices were carving a path of solitude and heartache.

In the crucible of her shattered dreams, Adveka painfully recognized the transformative power of her choices, but it was a transformation forced upon her by circumstances rather than a conscious act of empowerment. The invisible threads, woven with the harsh strands of karma and fate, painted a narrative not of resilience and self-discovery, but of a soul burdened by the consequences of unreciprocated love.

The chapters that lay ahead seemed more like a haunting continuation of her heartbreak, where the inevitable convergence of paths with Raivat appeared not as a beacon of hope but as a cruel twist of fate. As she moved forward, Adveka couldn't shake the feeling that the threads that bound her and Raivat were more like chains, pulling them back into a tragic dance orchestrated by forces beyond their control. The victimized Adveka trudged forward, her heart aching with the knowledge that the threads of karma and fate had woven a narrative where she was fated to bear the weight of unrequited love.

Chapter 2

Her Hiraeth

Kwan, a young man with a stable and strategic mind, navigated through life with a unique blend of precision and creativity. His mind, much like a well-constructed chessboard, always calculated the next move, ensuring that his decisions were not only thoughtful but also resilient. The world, to Kwan, was a vast chess game, and he positioned himself as the master strategist.

Dressed in a combination of black and blue, his attire mirrored his composed demeanor. The black symbolized the depth of his contemplative nature, while the blue reflected the vastness of his imagination. His wardrobe, much like his thoughts, was a canvas painted with the hues of intellect and creativity.

Kwan's exquisite taste extended beyond his wardrobe. He reveled in the finer things in life, appreciating the artistry of both tangible and intangible desires. Whether it was the pages of a well-written novel or the intricate details of a meticulously prepared dish, Kwan found pleasure in the refined aspects of the world. His ability to appreciate worldly beauty set him apart, making him a connoisseur of life's indulgences.

In the realm of friendships, Kwan stood as the perfect companion to Adveka, the duo having shared the tapestry of life for as long as they could remember. Their bond was not just a friendship; it was a harmonious blend of two minds complementing each other. Kwan's stability and strategic approach perfectly counterbalanced Adveka's spontaneity and adventurous spirit.

Despite their different paths in life, Kwan and Adveka remained steadfast friends. Kwan, with his meticulous mindset, had found his place in a world of numbers and logic, excelling in a career that demanded precision. Adveka, on the other hand, pursued a more dynamic and exploratory profession, but the differences in their occupations only served to enrich their friendship.

In the grand tapestry of life, Kwan was the thread that held the fabric together, weaving stability and strategy into the narrative. As the story unfolded, Kwan's presence became a testament to the enduring power of friendship and the beauty that could be found in the harmonious balance of differences.

Hanuel, the third spoke in this steadfast trinity, stood tall and proud as a master in the art of managing people. His charismatic demeanor and innate ability to understand human dynamics propelled him into the corporate world as a renowned manager. Hanuel, much like his name, which meant "sky" in Korean, had a personality that soared high, influencing those around him with his affable nature.

Having graduated alongside Adveka and Kwan, Hanuel embarked on a career that revolved around people. His success story resonated across boardrooms and lecture halls, inspiring aspiring business professionals to follow in his footsteps. With a magnetic presence and a natural flair for leadership, Hanuel had the uncanny ability to transform a group of individuals into a cohesive and efficient team.

As the trio journeyed from their college days into the complexities of adulthood, Hanuel's influence became evident not just in the corporate world but also within the tight-knit circle of friendship. He played the role of the glue, binding Adveka's adventurous spirit with Kwan's strategic mind. Hanuel's knack for handling people extended beyond the professional realm; it was the adhesive that kept their friendship intact.

Their paths diverged into distinct career trajectories, yet the camaraderie forged in college remained unbroken. Adveka explored uncharted territories, Kwan orchestrated the intricate moves, and Hanuel, with his managerial prowess, navigated the realm of human connections. The trio, each excelling in their own spheres, found solace and strength in the unwavering bond they had nurtured over the years.

In the grand narrative of their lives, Hanuel became the embodiment of leadership, not just within the corporate confines but also within the tapestry of their enduring friendship. His success story served as a beacon, illuminating the path for those who aspired to balance ambition with empathy.

As the chapters of their lives unfolded, the trio, Adveka, Kwan, and Hanuel, proved that while their individual journeys were diverse, the common thread of friendship, woven in the fabric of their college days, remained as resilient as ever. Their story continued to be a testament to the enduring power of camaraderie, proving that even as they ruled their respective worlds, the bond they shared was, and would always be, unbreakable.

As Adveka navigated the intricate dance of emotions, her heart weighed down by the unrequited love she harbored for Raivat, she found solace in the unwavering support of her two steadfast friends, Kwan and Hanuel. The bustling cityscape transformed into a refuge as the trio gathered in a cozy corner of their favorite coffee shop, where laughter and camaraderie had often been the backdrop to their stories.

Adveka, usually the epitome of adventurous spirit, now sat with a heavy heart, her eyes reflecting the pain of unfulfilled desires. Kwan's strategic mind and Hanuel's empathetic nature kicked into action as they recognized the need to lend a supportive ear to their dear friend.

In that familiar corner, amid the comforting aroma of coffee and the subtle hum of conversations, Adveka poured her heart out. The unspoken words of her one-sided love story found resonance in the sympathetic nods and understanding glances of Kwan and Hanuel. Their presence became a sanctuary, allowing Adveka to release the pent-up emotions that had been held captive within her.

Kwan, with his calm and composed demeanor, offered a strategic approach to healing. He shared insights on resilience, emphasizing the strength that could be drawn from within. Hanuel, on the other hand, provided a comforting embrace of understanding. His words were a balm to Adveka's wounded heart, reminding her that even in heartbreak, there was an opportunity for growth and self-discovery.

As the days unfolded, the trio engaged in various activities to lift Adveka's spirits. They embarked on spontaneous adventures, rediscovering the joy in simple pleasures. Kwan's meticulous planning ensured that every moment was a step towards healing, while Hanuel's contagious enthusiasm turned the mundane into moments of shared joy.

Through the ebb and flow of emotions, Adveka began to see the beauty in the support of true friends. The laughter that echoed through their shared moments became a powerful antidote to the ache in her heart. In their company, she discovered the strength to move forward, knowing that the tapestry of friendship could mend even the most delicate threads of the heart.

In this plot of resilience and friendship, Adveka's journey unfolded as a testament to the transformative power of companionship. Through the pain of unrequited love, she discovered that the bonds of true friendship could be a source of healing, mending the fractures with threads woven from understanding, laughter, and the enduring warmth of shared moments.

As Adveka stood at the crossroads of her career, the formidable duo of Kwan and Hanuel emerged not just as supportive friends but as invaluable assets, each contributing their unique expertise to shape the trajectory of her new venture.

Kwan, with his analytical mind and strategic acumen, undertook the role of the chief architect for Adveka's career transformation. Together, they meticulously devised a business plan that leveraged Adveka's strengths and passions. Kwan's knack for foreseeing challenges and devising effective solutions became the guiding force, ensuring that every step in Adveka's entrepreneurial journey was thoughtfully planned.

Hanuel, the maestro of managing people, transformed Adveka's professional landscape. With a network as vast as the sky he was named after, Hanuel connected Adveka with influential figures in the industry she aimed to conquer. His ability to foster relationships and create opportunities turned Adveka's venture into a collaborative effort that extended beyond her imagination.

Late-night brainstorming sessions became a cornerstone of their collaborative effort. Kwan's strategic mind and Hanuel's people skills blended seamlessly, as they delved into the intricacies of Adveka's business. Kwan's insights shaped the structure, ensuring stability and long-term viability, while Hanuel's connections facilitated crucial partnerships that fueled growth.

The coffee shop, now a bustling hub of ambition, witnessed the trio's dynamic collaboration. Kwan's spreadsheets and projections provided the roadmap, Hanuel's networking and management skills laid the foundation, and Adveka's determination and creativity infused life into their collective vision. The venture, which initially sprouted from Adveka's desire for change, metamorphosed into a collaborative masterpiece.

As the venture unfolded, Adveka found herself not just supported but elevated by the expertise of her friends. Kwan's strategic mind proved instrumental in navigating the complexities of the market, while Hanuel's people skills created a work environment that fostered creativity and innovation. The friendship between the three became the driving force, ensuring that Adveka's venture was not just a business but a manifestation of shared dreams.

In the grand tapestry of their collaboration, Adveka's friends became the cornerstone of her success. Kwan and Hanuel, with their strategic prowess and people-centric approach, turned the venture into a triumph of collective intelligence and shared ambitions. The story unfolded as a testament to the transformative power of friendship, where each friend's expertise seamlessly blended, shaping not just a career but a legacy of collaborative achievement.

As Adveka's venture gained momentum, the collaborative spirit among the trio intensified. Kwan's strategic mind continuously adapted the business model to evolving market dynamics, ensuring resilience in the face of challenges. Meanwhile, Hanuel's people skills created a work culture that fostered creativity and loyalty, making Adveka's venture not just a business but a community.

The coffee shop meetings transformed into bustling strategy sessions, with the trio synergizing their strengths. Kwan's financial models and market analyses became the foundation for informed decision-making, while Hanuel's team-building workshops cultivated a sense of purpose among Adveka's growing team. The venture, once a solo pursuit, had metamorphosed into a collaborative force driven by the shared expertise of the trio.

Adveka, now steering a ship guided by the combined brilliance of her friends, felt a newfound sense of empowerment. The trio's friendship had not only weathered the storm of heartbreak but had blossomed into a formidable alliance that transcended personal victories. Adveka's success was a testament to the strength derived from the collective wisdom and support of Kwan and Hanuel.

As the venture expanded, so did their individual roles within it. Kwan, with his eye for detail, managed the strategic alliances and financial aspects, ensuring the venture's growth remained sustainable. Hanuel, the master of people management, nurtured a positive work culture, attracting and retaining talented individuals who shared their passion.

Through highs and lows, the trio faced challenges head-on, relying on each other's strengths to navigate uncharted territories. Adveka's entrepreneurial journey became a story of friendship, resilience, and shared expertise, proving that when friends pool their talents, they can conquer even the most formidable obstacles.

The success of Adveka's venture didn't just echo within the business realm; it reverberated in their friendship, strengthening the bonds that had been forged in the crucible of college adventures. The trio's story became an inspiration, not just for aspiring entrepreneurs but for anyone seeking the transformative power of collaboration and steadfast friendship.

As the chapters of their intertwined lives continued to unfold, the friendship of Adveka, Kwan, and Hanuel stood as a testament to the enduring power of shared dreams, proving that when friends unite their expertise, they not only conquer professional challenges but also weave a narrative of lifelong support, growth, and triumph.

Adveka's venture, an emerging fashion jewelry brand, radiated with creativity, resilience, and the steadfast support of her friends, Kwan and Hanuel. The brand, named "MIRAB," symbolized a fusion of elegance, innovation, and Adveka's distinctive style, showcasing a radiant expression of her journey of self-discovery and transformation.

MIRAB sought to redefine the narrative of fashion jewelry, each piece meticulously crafted to reflect Adveka's artistic flair and Kwan's strategic insights into market trends. This jewelry line seamlessly blended modern aesthetics with timeless charm, appealing to a diverse audience seeking unique, statement pieces that embodied individuality.

Kwan's strategic acumen played a pivotal role in positioning MIRAB as a distinctive player in the competitive fashion industry. Through meticulous market analyses, Kwan identified niche opportunities, guiding the brand toward a strategic selection of materials, designs, and target demographics. The collaboration between Adveka's artistic vision and Kwan's strategic guidance resulted in a collection that transcended trends, resonating with those who valued jewelry as an expression of self.

Hanuel's people skills wove a thread of warmth into the fabric of MIRAB. The brand's success wasn't solely measured by its products but also by the inclusive and empowering work culture cultivated by Hanuel. The artisans and designers behind each piece weren't just employees; they were part of a creative family contributing to the brand's narrative with their unique talents.

MIRAB swiftly became a symbol of empowerment and self-expression, attracting a loyal following drawn to the authenticity of Adveka's journey and the brand's commitment to quality. The collaborative efforts of Adveka, Kwan, and Hanuel had transformed a dream into a reality, and MIRAB stood as a testament to the power of friendship and shared expertise.

The brand's story, intricately woven into the fabric of their lives, became a beacon for those who believed in the transformative potential of pursuing their passions. MIRAB wasn't just a jewelry brand; it was a manifestation of the resilience of Adveka, the strategic brilliance of Kwan, and the empathetic leadership of Hanuel. Together, they had created more than a business–they had birthed a movement that celebrated individuality, creativity, and the enduring strength found in true friendship.

Adveka's foray into the intricate world of finance became a cornerstone in the success story of MIRAB. Drawing on her newfound financial acumen, Adveka, with the strategic guidance of Kwan, navigated the complexities of budgeting, investments, and financial planning to propel MIRAB into international markets.

In the span of two years, Adveka's diligent financial strategies not only facilitated the brand's expansion overseas but also contributed significantly to overcoming the initial investment challenges. The careful allocation of resources, informed by Kwan's analytical insights, allowed MIRAB to establish a global presence while ensuring financial stability.

Kwan, leveraging his strategic mind, collaborated closely with Adveka to optimize financial decision-making. Together, they devised a meticulous expansion plan that considered market trends, currency fluctuations, and financial risk mitigation. Adveka's grasp of financial intricacies became instrumental in securing partnerships, managing cash flows, and navigating the regulatory landscapes of international markets.

As MIRAB gained a foothold overseas, the brand's profits soared exponentially, exceeding even the most optimistic projections. The financial success of the venture was a testament to the synergistic collaboration between Adveka's creative vision, Kwan's strategic financial planning, and Hanuel's people-centric leadership.

The trio's collective efforts had transformed MIRAB from a local gem to a global sensation. The financial success not only marked the triumph of Adveka's artistic vision but also showcased the transformative power of incorporating financial intelligence into the entrepreneurial journey. Adveka's perseverance, coupled with the strategic financial prowess of Kwan, and the supportive leadership of Hanuel, had turned MIRAB into a grand success.

MIRAB, now adorned by fashion enthusiasts around the world, stood as a testament to the enduring strength of friendship, the power of creative vision, and the strategic brilliance of financial planning. The journey, though challenging, had become a narrative of triumph, proving that with passion, strategic insight, and unwavering friendship, dreams could be transformed into a global reality.

Adveka's journey with MIRAB wasn't just a tale of financial triumph; it was a narrative of resilience in the face of personal adversity. Despite her own family disowning her for pursuing an unconventional path,

Adveka's determination only intensified. In these challenging moments, it was the unyielding support of her chosen family – Kwan and Hanuel – that became the bedrock of her strength.

Amidst the bustling offices and creative workshops, Adveka faced the harsh reality of familial estrangement. However, the void left by her family was seamlessly filled by the unwavering friendship and camaraderie of Kwan and Hanuel. They became her pillars of support, providing not only emotional solace but also practical assistance in building MIRAB from the ground up.

Adveka's nights were often spent not just sketching designs, but also navigating the complexities of entrepreneurship - from negotiating contracts to managing finances. Kwan, recognizing the gravity of her sacrifices, dedicated his strategic mind to streamline the business operations, ensuring every penny invested had a purpose and a promise of returns.

Hanuel's empathetic leadership played a pivotal role in fostering a work culture that served as a family for Adveka and her team. In the face of personal challenges, the trio transformed MIRAB into a haven of support, where creative minds flourished, and friendships thrived.

As the brand gained momentum and expanded globally, the financial success was not only a testament to Adveka's creative genius but also a tribute to the collective resilience of the trio. The challenges that came with being disowned by her family fueled Adveka's determination to prove that unconventional paths could lead to extraordinary destinations.

The success of MIRAB became a story of triumph over adversity, of a young woman who, with the support of true friends, turned rejection into a catalyst for success. The grand success of MIRAB wasn't just measured in profits; it was a testament to the indomitable spirit of Adveka, the strategic brilliance of Kwan, and the empathetic leadership of Hanuel.

In the world of fashion and entrepreneurship, MIRAB became more than a brand; it became a symbol of courage, perseverance, and the transformative power of friendship. Adveka's journey, though fraught with personal challenges, proved that with the right allies by one's side, dreams could not only be pursued but also surpassed, creating a legacy that went beyond familial boundaries.

As the global success of MIRAB continued to soar, Adveka found herself at the helm of a thriving empire that transcended the boundaries of fashion. The resilience that had fueled her journey from familial estrangement to entrepreneurial triumph became a beacon of inspiration for many aspiring individuals.

The trio's relentless dedication and the brand's international acclaim soon caught the attention of the fashion industry's elite. Adveka, once disowned for her unconventional choices, now stood at the forefront of innovation, breaking barriers and setting trends. The family she had chosen – Kwan and Hanuel – celebrated every milestone, their friendship becoming an unshakable foundation that withstood the tests of time.

MIRAB's success wasn't just a personal victory for Adveka; it was a testament to the transformative power of unwavering friendship. Kwan's strategic brilliance continued to steer the brand through financial waters, ensuring that every international venture was a calculated step towards sustainable growth. Hanuel's people-centric leadership created an organizational culture where passion and creativity flourished, making MIRAB not just a brand but a movement.

Amidst the glitz and glamour, Adveka remained grounded, always acknowledging the debt of gratitude she owed to her chosen family. The trio's journey, marked by adversity turned into triumph, resonated beyond the fashion industry, becoming a symbol of breaking societal norms and pursuing one's passion against all odds.

With the global expansion of MIRAB, Adveka decided to use her success to inspire others facing similar challenges. The brand initiated charitable projects supporting young artists and entrepreneurs, emphasizing the importance of resilience and camaraderie in the pursuit of dreams.

As MIRAB's legacy continued to unfold, the disapproval of Adveka's family seemed like a distant memory, overshadowed by the grandeur of her achievements. The brand, now synonymous with innovation and empowerment, had become a testament to the enduring strength of chosen families and the transformative journey from rejection to triumph.

In this tale of friendship, resilience, and unbridled success, Adveka, Kwan, and Hanuel stood united, their journey a testament to the fact that, in the grand tapestry of life, the threads of chosen family could weave a narrative of triumph and inspiration that transcended even the deepest wounds of rejection.

The pinnacle of Adveka's journey with MIRAB reached new heights as she secured the greatest opportunity of her career – a showcase at one of the world's most prestigious fashion shows, in partnership with a renowned fashion house. The prospect of having her creations grace the international runway was not just a validation of her talent but also a culmination of years of sleepless nights, relentless dedication, and unwavering determination.

In the weeks leading up to the grand event, Adveka immersed herself in the whirlwind of preparations. The sleepless nights were fueled not only by the need for perfection but also by the vision of MIRAB capturing the hearts of a global audience. Kwan's strategic mind played a crucial role in navigating the complexities of marketing and exposure, ensuring that every facet of the brand was highlighted to its fullest potential.

The day of the fashion show arrived, a culmination of dreams and hard work. Adveka's creations, reflecting her unique blend of creativity and innovation, dazzled on the runway. The applause that echoed through the venue was not just for the fashion house but for the resilience of a young entrepreneur who had defied the odds.

The success of the show propelled MIRAB into the elite league of fashion houses, earning the brand a coveted spot among the listed ones. The accolades, media attention, and international recognition poured in, transforming MIRAB from a brand with a story into a global phenomenon.

Amidst the newfound glory, Adveka never lost sight of her roots. The trio, bound by the threads of enduring friendship, celebrated the triumph together. The essence of MIRAB remained rooted in the values that had propelled its inception - creativity, resilience, and the unwavering support of true friends.

Adveka's success didn't create a divide; instead, it strengthened the bond between her and Kwan and Hanuel. The trio, though now managing a globally acclaimed brand, continued to navigate life's journey with the same camaraderie that had defined their college days. Success, for Adveka, was not just a personal triumph but a shared victory with the friends who had stood by her through thick and thin.

The anticipation in the air was palpable as Adveka prepared for MIRAB's grand showcase at the world-renowned fashion show. The glitz and glamour of the event didn't overshadow the sleepless nights and tireless efforts that had gone into every intricate detail of the success shoe. Adveka, fueled by passion and determination, worked ceaselessly to ensure that each piece told a story – a narrative of resilience, creativity, and the journey that had brought MIRAB to this pivotal moment.

The runway itself became a canvas for Adveka's artistic expression. The success shoe was carefully choreographed to unfold like a captivating tale, with each piece of jewelry taking center stage, telling its own chapter in the narrative of MIRAB. Kwan's strategic insights came to life as the marketing and presentation of each creation reflected a meticulous understanding of the global fashion landscape.

The venue was a symphony of lights and colors, a testament to the fusion of Adveka's artistic vision and Kwan's strategic brilliance. The media buzz surrounding MIRAB's showcase was unprecedented, drawing attention not just to the brand but to the story behind its meteoric rise. The success shoe became a spectacle that transcended fashion, symbolizing a journey of determination and triumph over adversity.

Adveka, clad in a creation of her own, took a bow as the applause reverberated through the venue. The success shoe had not only showcased MIRAB's collection but had also created a moment of profound recognition for the young entrepreneur who had turned rejection into a global triumph.

The aftermath of the success shoe was nothing short of spectacular. MIRAB's designs adorned the pages of international fashion magazines, the brand's social media platforms buzzed with admiration, and the demand for Adveka's creations reached unprecedented levels. The success shoe had not just launched a collection; it had launched MIRAB into the upper echelons of the fashion industry.

As accolades and partnerships poured in, Kwan and Hanuel stood by Adveka, their camaraderie solidifying into an unbreakable bond of shared success. The success shoe had not only opened doors for MIRAB but had also become a chapter in the ongoing story of friendship and triumph that the trio continued to write.

The success shoe wasn't just an event; it was a defining moment in the MIRAB narrative. It underscored the brand's ability to weave dreams into tangible creations, proving that behind the glimmering jewels and glamorous runway was a tale of resilience, hard work, and the enduring strength of friendship. Adveka's success shoe wasn't just a showcase; it was a statement – a declaration to the world that MIRAB had arrived, and it was here to stay.

In the grand narrative of MIRAB's success, Adveka's commitment to her roots became a beacon of authenticity. Despite the glitz and glamour of the international stage, she remained grounded, always acknowledging the contributions of her chosen family in the journey towards triumph.

The story of MIRAB became a living testament to the enduring power of friendship and the idea that, no matter how high one soars, staying connected to one's roots and true companions ensures that success is not just an individual achievement but a shared legacy of love, resilience, and unbreakable bonds.

As MIRAB's success reverberated across borders, the brand swiftly became a global sensation, gracing the shelves of high-end boutiques and capturing the hearts of fashion enthusiasts in different countries. Adveka's artistic brilliance, coupled with Kwan's strategic mind and Hanuel's people-centric leadership, turned MIRAB into a household name in the business field.

The international expansion became a testament to the universal appeal of MIRAB's designs. Adveka's creations, inspired by diverse cultures and influenced by her own journey, resonated with individuals from various corners of the world. The brand's popularity surged, not just for its exquisite jewelry but for the empowering narrative it represented – a narrative of perseverance, creativity, and the enduring strength of friendship.

Kwan, leveraging his strategic expertise, navigated the complexities of global markets, ensuring that MIRAB's expansion was not just rapid but also sustainable. Collaborations with international retailers, exclusive showcases at prestigious events, and strategic partnerships with influential figures in the fashion industry became the norm, solidifying MIRAB's position as a trailblazer in the business field.

Hanuel's people-centric approach played a crucial role in building a diverse and passionate team, ensuring that MIRAB's global success was not just a triumph for the founders but a collective achievement. The brand's success was not measured solely by financial gains but by the positive impact it had on the lives of those associated with it – from the artisans crafting each piece to the fashion enthusiasts who adorned themselves with MIRAB's creations.

The media hailed MIRAB as a success story, not just in the fashion industry but in the broader business landscape. Adveka, Kwan, and Hanuel were lauded for their entrepreneurial acumen, turning a small venture into a global enterprise in record time. The trio became sought-after speakers at international business conferences, sharing their insights on innovation, collaboration, and the transformative power of friendship in the business world.

MIRAB's headquarters, once a modest workshop, now stood as a symbol of entrepreneurial triumph. The brand's impact extended beyond fashion, inspiring aspiring entrepreneurs to chase their dreams relentlessly. Adveka, the creative force behind MIRAB, remained true to her roots, always acknowledging the integral roles that Kwan and Hanuel played in the brand's meteoric rise.

In boardrooms and fashion capitals alike, MIRAB emerged as a new name in the business field, a beacon of success that showcased the unlimited possibilities of passion, resilience, and unwavering friendship. The brand's global triumph was not just a chapter in the trio's story; it was a narrative that echoed the belief that, with creativity, collaboration, and genuine connections, entrepreneurs could transcend borders and redefine success in ways unimaginable.

The dazzling success of MIRAB faced an unexpected and devastating twist as Adveka encountered betrayal from one of her managing directors. The blow was not just financial; it struck at the core of trust and camaraderie that had been pivotal to MIRAB's journey. Despite her unwavering faith in her team, Adveka found herself grappling with the harsh reality of deception.

The betrayal sent shockwaves through the organization, and the distress Adveka felt was palpable. Her friends, Kwan and Hanuel, rallied around her, determined to curb the losses and salvage what they could. Late-night strategy sessions and crisis meetings became the norm, but the financial intricacies of the situation seemed insurmountable, even for Adveka's astute mind.

For the first time in her career, Adveka found herself in a position of helplessness. The weight of the betrayal was compounded by the responsibility she felt toward her dedicated team and the brand she had nurtured with passion. The trio, once an impenetrable force, now faced an unprecedented challenge that shook the foundations of MIRAB.

As the losses mounted, Adveka, with a heavy heart, contemplated difficult decisions – restructuring, downsizing, or even the possibility of selling a stake in the brand. The magnitude of the crisis seemed to eclipse the resilience that had defined MIRAB's journey so far.

The echoes of betrayal reverberated through the once vibrant halls of MIRAB, casting a shadow over the brand's triumphant history. Adveka, with a heavy heart, confronted the harsh reality of the situation. The loyalty she had placed in her managing director had been shattered, and the financial repercussions were severe.

Despite the unwavering support of Kwan and Hanuel, the trio found themselves entangled in a web of financial complexity that seemed insurmountable. Late-night strategy sessions and crisis meetings became a desperate attempt to salvage the brand they had built from the ground up. The once-thriving atmosphere of creativity and innovation now seemed tainted by the betrayal that had disrupted the harmony.

As losses continued to accumulate, Adveka faced the daunting task of making decisions that would shape MIRAB's future. The weight of responsibility bore down on her shoulders, and the trio grappled with the possibility of restructuring, downsizing, or other drastic measures. The resilient spirit that had fueled their journey now faced its sternest test.

The void left by the betrayal remained palpable, creating a sense of uncertainty that permeated the once-confident halls of MIRAB's headquarters. Adveka's financially educated mind, while formidable, seemed momentarily powerless against the intricate web of deceit and financial turmoil.

In this moment of crisis, the future of MIRAB hung in the balance, and the closure of this chapter in the brand's narrative remained open-ended. The uncertainty of what lies ahead lingers, leaving the story poised for a new chapter, one that could either spell redemption or further challenges for Adveka, Kwan, and Hanuel. The void, as yet unfilled, awaits the unfolding of the next chapter in the tumultuous journey of MIRAB.

Chapter 3

Initti Affiniti

In the midst of MIRAB's tumultuous chapter, a new character emerged on the horizon, introducing an air of mystery and expertise to the narrative. Yichen, a figure shrouded in a cloak of enigma, entered the scene with an aura of confidence and a track record of transforming struggling businesses into flourishing enterprises.

Yichen, with his commanding presence, walked into MIRAB's headquarters with the assurance of a king surveying his realm. His deep understanding of the business world and an uncanny ability to think outside the conventional boundaries marked him as a formidable force. Yichen's unique talent lay in unraveling intricate problems, finding solutions where others saw only challenges, and breathing new life into seemingly dying ventures.

Known for his knack for acquiring struggling businesses and turning them into success stories, Yichen brought a fresh perspective to the table. His entrance into MIRAB's narrative raised eyebrows and stirred curiosity among those who had weathered the storm of betrayal. Adveka, Kwan, and Hanuel, though wary, couldn't help but feel a glimmer of hope in Yichen's potential to lead them out of the current crisis.

Yichen's reputation as someone who hunted down foes with a crushing attitude intrigued those who witnessed his entrance. The mere mention of his name sent ripples through the business world, signifying a force to be reckoned with. As he walked through the halls of MIRAB, his steps resonated with the confidence of someone who had navigated countless challenges and emerged victorious.

Amidst the uncertainty, Yichen's presence introduced an element of intrigue and potential salvation. As the quartet – Adveka, Kwan, Hanuel, and now Yichen – began to strategize, the dynamics of MIRAB's story took an unexpected turn. The void left by betrayal seemed to tremble in the wake of Yichen's entrance, setting the stage for a new chapter in the tumultuous journey of MIRAB.

Adveka, amidst the chaos caused by betrayal and financial turmoil, found herself at a crossroads. The arrival of Yichen, with his commanding presence and a reputation for resurrecting businesses, stirred a mixture of curiosity and cautious optimism. Adveka, recognizing the dire straits of MIRAB, realized that cooperation with Yichen might be the key to salvaging the brand she had painstakingly built.

The weight of the impending meeting with Yichen bore down on Adveka's shoulders as she navigated the labyrinthine corridors of uncertainty. The struggle to secure this pivotal encounter was a testament to her unwavering determination to save MIRAB at any cost.

Amidst the chaos of betrayal and financial turmoil, Adveka faced countless obstacles in arranging the meeting with Yichen. Negotiations, rescheduling, and navigating the intricate web of business dynamics consumed her days and nights. Yet, with each setback, her resolve only strengthened. The future of MIRAB hung in the balance, and Adveka, with her financially educated mind, understood the urgency of this collaboration.

In the face of mounting challenges, Adveka's pursuit of the meeting resembled a relentless odyssey. She fought through bureaucratic red tape, endured sleepless nights to draft compelling proposals, and exhibited a tenacity that mirrored the spirit that had propelled MIRAB to success. The corridors of power and influence became a battleground, and Adveka emerged as a warrior, driven by the singular goal of securing Yichen's cooperation.

The struggle extended beyond logistical hurdles. Adveka found herself confronting doubts, both internal and external, about the wisdom of partnering with someone as enigmatic as Yichen. Whispers of skepticism lingered in the air, but Adveka remained resolute, her focus fixed on the salvation of MIRAB.

The day of the meeting arrived, and Adveka, adorned in the very creations that embodied MIRAB's essence, exuded a quiet confidence. The stakes were high, and as she stepped into the room where Yichen awaited, the weight of anticipation filled the air. The aura of determination around Adveka was palpable, a silent declaration that she would leave no stone unturned to rescue her brand.

The struggle to reach this pivotal moment had been an arduous journey, fraught with challenges that tested Adveka's resilience. The meeting with Yichen became a turning point, a moment of reckoning where the fate of MIRAB would be shaped. As Adveka, with a steely gaze, took her seat at the table, the struggle that brought her here underscored the depth of her commitment and the lengths to which she was willing to go to ensure the survival and success of MIRAB.

The meeting room was charged with an undercurrent of tension as Adveka, Kwan, and Hanuel sat across from Yichen. The air hung heavy with unspoken questions and expectations, each participant gauging the other's intentions. Adveka's financially educated mind, usually a wellspring of strategic acumen, worked overtime as she sought to navigate the complexities of this critical encounter.

Yichen, with an air of calculated confidence, observed the trio before him. His gaze, sharp and discerning, seemed to pierce through the surface, assessing not just the individuals seated across from him but the essence of MIRAB itself. The dynamics in the room echoed the high stakes and the potential for a transformative alliance.

Adveka, the linchpin of MIRAB's journey, initiated the conversation, her tone a blend of poise and urgency. She articulated the challenges that had beset the brand, laying bare the extent of the betrayal and the financial turmoil that threatened to engulf MIRAB. Yichen listened attentively, his expressions unreadable, but the wheels of his mind undoubtedly turning.

As the dialogue unfolded, Adveka strategically steered the conversation towards the potential collaboration. She highlighted Yichen's track record of turning around struggling businesses, emphasizing how his unique talents could be the lifeline MIRAB desperately needed. The financial intricacies were dissected, and Adveka's financially educated mind found resonance in Yichen's astute observations.

Kwan and Hanuel, loyal pillars of support, contributed their perspectives, underlining the importance of trust and synergy in MIRAB's journey. The quartet engaged in a delicate dance of words, each sentence carrying the weight of MIRAB's past, present, and potential future. The atmosphere, though tense, crackled with the anticipation of a pivotal decision that could redefine the trajectory of the brand.

Yichen, the enigmatic force in the room, remained composed, his responses measured and calculated. His questions, probing and insightful, revealed a keen understanding of MIRAB's industry, its challenges, and the potential avenues for revival. The meeting became a strategic chess match, with each move calculated to secure an alliance that could either breathe new life into MIRAB or lead to its demise.

As the meeting drew to a close, an air of uncertainty lingered. Adveka, Kwan, and Hanuel departed, leaving Yichen to deliberate on the proposal. The room, now devoid of voices, held the echoes of a crucial encounter that could either mark the beginning of MIRAB's resurgence or a chapter of further challenges. The fate of MIRAB hung in the balance, and the next steps remained shrouded in the uncertainty of Yichen's decision.

As the discussion unfolded, Adveka began to see the potential synergy between Yichen's out-of-the-box thinking and her strategic vision. Yichen's past successes spoke volumes, and Adveka, despite her initial reservations, began to consider the prospect of collaboration. It became evident that their skills, when combined, could create a formidable force capable of steering MIRAB away from the brink of collapse.

The decision to cooperate with Yichen was not made lightly. Adveka, driven by the determination to save MIRAB, extended an olive branch, recognizing the expertise Yichen could bring to the table. The quartet, now united in purpose, embarked on a journey to navigate the intricacies of betrayal, financial challenges, and the uncertain future that loomed over MIRAB.

As the story unfolds, the question of whether Yichen will help Adveka and the fate of MIRAB remains uncertain. The dynamics of this newfound collaboration, with its potential for redemption or further challenges, hang in the balance. The journey of MIRAB, now intertwined with the enigmatic Yichen, is poised for a dramatic turn, leaving readers to wonder whether Yichen will emerge as the savior or a new challenge in the turbulent narrative of MIRAB's journey.

Yichen, having listened attentively to Adveka's impassioned plea and the intricate details of MIRAB's challenges, leaned back in his chair. The room, once filled with the palpable tension of strategic negotiations, now echoed with the weight of Adveka's heartfelt request. His sharp gaze lingered on Adveka, whose eyes bore the desperation of a leader fighting to preserve her creation.

As the conversation took an unexpected turn, Adveka, with sincerity etched in her voice, implored Yichen not to adhere to his principle of acquisition. Her plea was raw and genuine, a plea to salvage the essence of MIRAB without subsuming it into the Yichen Group. The financial intricacies were replaced with a more profound appeal – the preservation of a dream that had transcended mere business.

Yichen, known for his calculated decisions and ruthless business tactics, found himself facing an unfamiliar crossroad. Adveka's request struck a chord that resonated beyond the realm of profit margins and acquisitions. He observed the genuine passion in Adveka's eyes, the fervent plea to save not just a business but a labor of love, a testament to her creativity and resilience.

As Adveka's words lingered in the air, Yichen contemplated the significance of this moment. The meeting, initially a discussion of business intricacies, had transformed into a human narrative, one where the fate of MIRAB intertwined with the emotions and aspirations of its founder. Yichen, a master of strategy, found himself confronted with a decision that transcended the rigid confines of his business principles.

The room fell into a momentary silence, the weight of the impending decision hanging in the air. Yichen, a figure known for his stoic demeanor, revealed little of the internal deliberations transpiring within him. Adveka's eyes, filled with a mix of anxiety and hope, remained fixed on Yichen, waiting for a response that could determine the destiny of MIRAB.

As the pivotal meeting hung in the balance, Yichen's phone vibrated urgently on the conference table. He glanced at the screen and a shadow crossed his face. The room, filled with anticipation, witnessed a rare vulnerability in Yichen's composed demeanor. Without a word, he excused himself and hastily exited the meeting room.

Adveka, Kwan, and Hanuel exchanged glances, the uncertainty of the situation deepening. Yichen's abrupt departure left the trio in a state of suspended animation, the fate of MIRAB momentarily forgotten in the face of a personal crisis. The open end of the story now pivoted to an unforeseen development that transcended the realms of business negotiations.

Outside the meeting room, Yichen navigated the bustling corridors with a palpable urgency. His thoughts, initially consumed by the negotiations, were now overtaken by concern for his mother. The news of her accident had shattered the carefully constructed walls around Yichen's emotions, revealing a vulnerability that few had witnessed.

As Yichen hurriedly made his way to the hospital, a myriad of emotions churned within him. The urgency of his mother's situation eclipsed the strategic negotiations he had just been part of. The enigmatic figure known for decisive business moves now found himself at the mercy of an unforeseen personal crisis.

At the hospital, Yichen received the distressing details - his mother, in need of immediate blood transfusion, required a rare blood type, AB negative. The urgency of the situation prompted Yichen to step into action. He contacted his network, mobilizing resources to secure the required blood for his mother.

Yichen's personal crisis introduces a new layer of complexity, leaving the trio - Adveka, Kwan, and Hanuel - in a state of uncertainty. The question now remains: Will Yichen's priorities shift, and how will the events at the hospital influence the trajectory of MIRAB's future? The narrative stands at the cusp of an unpredictable turn, waiting for the next chapter to unfold.

The urgency in the hospital staff's voice resonated through Adveka's phone, cutting through the intense atmosphere of the conference room. She glanced at Kwan and Hanuel, her expression a mix of determination and concern. Without a moment's hesitation, she excused herself, leaving the room with a sense of purpose that overshadowed the complexities of MIRAB's situation.

In the corridors outside the conference room, Adveka's swift steps mirrored the urgency of the call. Her mind, initially consumed by the intricacies of business negotiations, now shifted gears to a more immediate, altruistic cause. The hospital became her destination, a place where the rarity of her blood type transformed her into a potential savior.

As she made her way to the hospital, Adveka's thoughts were momentarily detached from the financial turmoil plaguing MIRAB. The altruistic act of donating her rare blood became a priority, a testament to her unwavering commitment to humanity in the face of personal and professional challenges.

The hospital, with its stark white walls and bustling corridors, welcomed Adveka into a different kind of battlefield. The urgency in her steps mirrored the urgency of the situation, her determination undeterred by the uncertainties that loomed over MIRAB. Adveka, clad in the very creations that embodied MIRAB's essence, became a beacon of hope in the midst of her own company's storm.

The scene unfolded as Adveka entered the blood donation center, a realm of selflessness amid the chaos of life's unpredictabilities. The hospital staff guided her to a room where the act of giving transcended business complexities. Adveka's decision to leave for the hospital, driven by a higher purpose, emphasized her ability to compartmentalize and prioritize humanity over the immediate challenges her company faced.

In a room filled with the sterile scent of hospitals, Yichen paced nervously, his phone clutched tightly in his hand. The news about his mother's accident had cast a shadow over his composed demeanor, revealing a vulnerability seldom seen. The urgency of the situation weighed heavily on his shoulders as he awaited crucial updates.

Just as anxiety threatened to consume him, the phone vibrated with a relieving call. The hospital staff delivered the news he had been desperately hoping for - a donor with AB negative blood had been located, and the necessary arrangements were underway. A surge of relief flooded through Yichen, momentarily dispelling the cloud of worry that had enveloped him.

As he processed the information, Yichen felt a profound gratitude towards the anonymous donor who, unbeknownst to him, had stepped forward to save his mother's life. The news brought a momentary reprieve from the emotional tumult, allowing him to focus on the logistics of ensuring the swift transfusion his mother needed.

In the hospital corridors, Yichen made his way to the blood transfusion center, guided by the hospital staff. The significance of the moment wasn't lost on him - the availability of blood meant a potential lifeline for his mother, and he moved with a purpose that mirrored the urgency of the situation.

Unaware of the unfolding events around him, Yichen entered the realm of medical procedures and life-saving measures. The hospital staff, efficient and compassionate, ushered him through the corridors, heading towards the room where the anonymous donor awaited, ready to contribute a precious gift – the gift of life.

As Adveka lay connected to the blood transfusion lines, a silent exchange of glances occurred between her and Yichen. The hospital room, with its clinical white walls and hushed tones, became the stage for an unspoken connection that transcended the complexities of their professional lives.

Yichen, initially observing the medical procedure with a sense of gratitude, found his gaze drawn towards Adveka. Their eyes met in a moment of unexpected clarity, a pause in the hurried rhythm of life that spoke volumes without uttering a single word. In that instant, the boundaries of business negotiations and corporate strategies dissolved, revealing a shared vulnerability and humanity.

Adveka, focused on the act of giving, felt the weight of Yichen's gaze. The exchange of eye contact became a bridge between their worlds, a connection forged in the midst of a life-saving gesture. The silent acknowledgment in their eyes conveyed a mutual understanding that, in this moment, they were bound by something greater than the intricacies of MIRAB or the twists of fate that had brought them here.

The hospital room, for that brief moment, held the essence of shared humanity. The unspoken language between Adveka and Yichen echoed the complexity of their intertwined destinies. In the midst of medical procedures and life-altering moments, their eyes exchanged a silent agreement – an acknowledgment that, beyond the veneer of business personas, they were both participants in a shared narrative that extended beyond the hospital room.

As Yichen stood there, his eyes locked with Adveka's in the quiet hospital room, a profound shift occurred within him. The silent exchange of glances, the unspoken understanding of shared vulnerability and compassion, kindled an unexpected spark. In that moment, the complexities of business negotiations faded away, leaving behind the raw essence of their shared humanity.

As the blood transfusion continued, Yichen found himself captivated by Adveka's sense of responsibility. Her altruistic act, not only saving his mother's life but also extending a lifeline to a stranger, resonated deeply with him. Adveka's unwavering commitment to humanity, even in the face of her challenges, ignited a newfound admiration within Yichen.

The realization dawned on him that there was more to this moment than the intricacies of MIRAB. A desire to reciprocate Adveka's selflessness stirred within Yichen. He contemplated the possibility of extending a helping hand to her company, not just as a strategic move, but as a genuine gesture born out of admiration for her resilience and sense of responsibility.

In the days that followed, Yichen, still processing the unexpected twist of fate, found himself reflecting on the nature of their encounter. The hospital room had become a catalyst for a deeper connection, one that went beyond the boardrooms and business negotiations. As he mulled over the idea of assisting Adveka with MIRAB, a realization dawned on him – he had fallen in love with her not just for her business acumen but for the strength of character that shone through in moments of adversity.

Chapter 4

Innombrable Dastan

In the aftermath of the unexpected encounter at the hospital, Yichen's mind became a canvas painted with thoughts of Adveka. The silent exchange of glances had stirred emotions and reflections that transcended the confines of business negotiations, prompting Yichen to reevaluate the nature of their connection. As he delved into his own introspections, a profound realization dawned – Adveka might be the perfect woman for him.

Adveka's immediate and altruistic response to the urgent call for blood donation left an indelible mark on Yichen. Her unwavering commitment to humanity, coupled with her sense of responsibility towards others, resonated deeply with him. Yichen, who had been searching for a partner with a similar passion for business and a shared commitment to making a positive impact, saw in Adveka the embodiment of these qualities.

Adveka's fire and passion, not only for the intricacies of the business world but also for humanitarian causes, aligned seamlessly with Yichen's own values. The hospital room, where their paths had converged, symbolized a shared world where success in the corporate realm intertwined with a genuine commitment to the well-being of others.

Envisioning a future with Adveka, Yichen saw the potential for a partnership that extended beyond mere business ventures. He imagined a dynamic where they could elevate each other both professionally and embark on joint endeavors that made a meaningful impact on society. The prospect of a life with Adveka brought a sense of excitement and possibility, unleashing a flame within Yichen that went beyond the calculated mindset he applied to his business endeavors.

As Yichen considered the evolving nature of his feelings, he envisioned a romantic and professional journey with Adveka that could redefine both their lives and the trajectory of MIRAB. The open end of the story now lies in Yichen's contemplations and the unfolding possibilities of their connection, leaving readers to speculate about the uncharted territory and the potential for love and success that awaits.

In the days that followed the serendipitous encounter at the hospital, Yichen found himself driven by a newfound determination to bring life back to MIRAB and, in turn, to support Adveka. Without waiting for further requests, he took the reins of the situation and devised a comprehensive plan to rejuvenate the struggling fashion jewelry brand.

Yichen's strategic mind, honed by years of navigating the intricacies of the business world, went to work. He meticulously analyzed the challenges that MIRAB faced, identified key areas of improvement, and formulated a revitalization strategy. His goal was not merely to salvage the company but to elevate it to new heights, showcasing the resilience and innovation that had made MIRAB successful in the past.

The business tycoon, known for his dominance in the corporate landscape, brought forth a plan that demonstrated his prowess and established his superiority once again. Yichen orchestrated strategic partnerships, implemented innovative marketing campaigns, and infused fresh energy into MIRAB's product lines. His vision extended beyond mere business transactions - he aimed to breathe life into the brand and, by extension, uplift Adveka in her time of need.

Yichen's actions were swift and calculated, reflecting his commitment to not only revive MIRAB but also to align it with contemporary market trends. He leveraged his vast network, drawing on connections built over years of successful business ventures, to position MIRAB as a formidable player in the fashion jewelry industry once again.

As the revitalization plan unfolded, Adveka witnessed the transformation orchestrated by Yichen. The dominance he exhibited in the boardrooms seamlessly translated into a reinvigorated brand identity for MIRAB. Yichen's unwavering determination to see Adveka back on her feet became apparent as he steered the company toward a resurgence that surpassed expectations.

The city's vibrant lights were beginning to flicker on as the day made way for the twilight hours. Adveka, wrapped up in the rhythm of her own thoughts, received an unexpected message – a cryptic warning of danger that sent shivers down her spine.

Adveka's heart raced, and a knot tightened in her stomach as she realized the severity of the impending danger. She couldn't reach him in time to prevent the orchestrated accident from unfolding.

The scene erupted into chaos as the assailants lunged at Yichen. The orchestrated accident unfolded with ruthless efficiency – a calculated assault meant to incapacitate the usually composed business tycoon. Adveka's steps quickened into a sprint, desperation etched across her face as she fought against time.

And then, the world seemed to freeze for Adveka. Yichen, the formidable figure of success, crumpled to the ground under the force of the assault. The air was filled with a sickening thud as Yichen's body collided with the cold pavement. A pool of crimson seeped from the wounds inflicted, staining the ground beneath him.

As Yichen lay unconscious in the dimly lit alley, the orchestrated accident had left him battered and vulnerable. His usually composed demeanor was shattered, and the pool of crimson around him marked the aftermath of a calculated assault. The cold pavement beneath him served as an unforgiving testament to the brutality he had endured. The shadows that once concealed the assailants now bore witness to the aftermath of their sinister plan.

Adveka, propelled by an urgent sense of fear and a gut feeling that refused to be ignored, rushed to Yichen's side. The city, usually alive with activity, had taken on an eerie stillness as if holding its breath, mirroring Adveka's own heightened anxiety. As she knelt beside him, the gravity of the situation hit her with a visceral force. Yichen, the indomitable figure of success, now lay unconscious, his life hanging in the balance.

The metallic scent of blood hung heavy in the air as Adveka's trembling hands checked for signs of life. Yichen's once sharp features were now disfigured by the brutality of the orchestrated accident. The vulnerability of the moment sent shockwaves through Adveka, and a deep-seated fear clawed at her insides. The person before her wasn't just a strategic partner; he was someone she had come to care about deeply.

Her voice wavered as she urgently called for help, the desperation cutting through the silence of the night. Paramedics arrived, their professionalism taking over the scene. However, Adveka's eyes remained fixed on Yichen. The weight of the moment lingered, and amidst the chaos, she grappled with emotions that surpassed the calculated world of business.

In that dimly lit alley, surrounded by the aftermath of violence, Adveka's perspective shifted. The fear of losing Yichen had unveiled a depth of emotion she hadn't fully acknowledged until that night. Love, unexpected and unspoken, began to blossom in her heart. Yichen, once a strategic partner, had become someone she couldn't bear to lose – someone for whom her heart now beat in a different rhythm.

The antiseptic scent of the hospital greeted Adveka as she stepped into the sterile environment, the harsh fluorescent lights casting a cold glow on the hallway. The rhythmic beeping of medical equipment echoed through the corridor, each sounds a stark reminder of the battle Yichen was fighting for his life.

Entering the intensive care unit, Adveka's heart clenched at the sight that unfolded before her. Yichen lay motionless on the hospital bed, surrounded by a web of tubes and wires. His once impeccable appearance was now replaced by a vulnerability that struck Adveka to the core.

Yichen's face, though partially obscured by bandages, bore the evidence of the orchestrated accident's brutality. The gauges and pipes connected to his body painted a vivid picture of the intricate fight for survival happening within him. The sterile white sheets clung to his form, and the room seemed to hold its breath as the medical equipment continued its steady symphony.

Adveka approached the bedside, her eyes fixed on Yichen's pale face. The beeping of the heart monitor created a haunting backdrop to the silent plea she whispered to the universe. She felt a lump forming in her throat as she fought to hold back tears, her fingers gently gripping Yichen's hand, seeking solace in the warmth that remained.

As Adveka bowed her head in a silent prayer, her thoughts and emotions intertwined in a desperate plea for the life she cherished the most. The sterile hospital room became a sacred space where hope and fear coexisted, and time seemed to stretch, suspended in the uncertainty of Yichen's fate.

The hum of the machines, the distant footsteps of medical personnel, and the muted sounds of the outside world all faded into the background as Adveka poured her heart into the silent communion with the divine. She prayed for strength, for healing, and for a chance to see Yichen's eyes open once more.

In those vulnerable moments, Adveka found herself grappling with the fragility of life and the unpredictable turns it could take. The hospital room, usually a place of healing, now stood as a battleground between life and the looming specter of loss.

As Adveka continued to stand by Yichen's bedside, her silent prayers echoed in the sterile confines of the intensive care unit. The hum of the medical equipment created a dissonant melody, underscoring the uncertainty that permeated the room. The rhythmic beeping of the heart monitor seemed to dictate the fragile dance between life and the looming specter of loss.

Her fingers intertwined with Yichen's, Adveka found solace in the warmth that lingered. She traced the contours of his hand, her touch gentle as she sought to convey a silent reassurance that transcended the clinical surroundings. The sterile white walls seemed to close in on her, and each passing second felt like an eternity as she awaited any sign of life from the man who had become more than just a strategic partner.

The beeping of the heart monitor, though steady, added an ominous rhythm to the room. Adveka's gaze remained fixed on Yichen's face, hidden beneath bandages and gauges. His stillness contrasted sharply with the vitality that usually defined him. The bustling hospital became a sacred space where Adveka confronted the fragility of life, her emotions swirling in a tempest of hope, fear, and an unspoken acknowledgment of the love that had silently blossomed.

The medical staff moved around with practiced efficiency, their words exchanged in hushed tones, leaving Adveka feeling like a mere spectator in a surreal drama. Her thoughts, however, were a tumultuous sea of emotions – memories of shared laughter, challenging negotiations, and the unspoken connection that had grown between them.

The uncertainty of Yichen's fate loomed large, and Adveka grappled with the weight of the unknown. In those quiet moments, she allowed herself to acknowledge the depth of her feelings. Love had found its way into her heart amidst the chaos of the orchestrated accident, and now it lingered in the hospital room, tangled with the uncertainty of the future.

As the minutes stretched into hours, Adveka found herself caught between the realms of hope and despair. She prayed not just for Yichen's life but for the chance to explore the uncharted territory of their evolving connection. The hospital room, with its stark white walls and mechanical sounds, became a crucible of emotions, and Adveka stood at its center, grappling with the fragility of life and the unpredictability of love.

Time seemed to stretch endlessly in the sterile confines of the intensive care unit, each moment laden with the weight of anticipation. Adveka continued to stand vigil by Yichen's bedside, her heart a battleground where hope and the looming specter of heartbreak engaged in a silent struggle.

The hospital room, once a symbol of healing, now encapsulated the fragility of life and the emotional tumult that Adveka grappled with. Her gaze never wavered from Yichen's face, obscured by bandages and gauges, as if willing him to awaken from the silent depths of unconsciousness. She yearned for the resumption of the vitality that had defined him, for the warmth of his gaze to dispel the coldness that lingered in the room.

The beeping of the heart monitor remained a steady but haunting accompaniment to Adveka's thoughts. Each beat seemed to underscore the delicate balance between hope and despair, amplifying the uncertainty that enveloped the hospital room. As she stood there, emotions intertwined like an intricate tapestry, Adveka found herself confronting not only the potential loss of a cherished life but also the awakening of a love she hadn't expected.

In the midst of this emotional turmoil, Adveka replayed moments from their shared journey – the triumphs, the challenges, and the unspoken connection that had quietly blossomed. Love, once a subtle undercurrent, now surged within her, its presence undeniable in the face of potential heartbreak. The hospital room became a crucible of conflicting emotions, where the line between hope and despair blurred.

The medical staff, with their clinical efficiency, moved around Adveka, offering reassurances that felt hollow against the backdrop of uncertainty. She clung to Yichen's hand, as if the warmth could bridge the gap between unconsciousness and awakening. Her silent prayers echoed in the sterile air, a plea for a second chance not just at life but at exploring the depths of this unexpected love.

As the minutes turned into hours, Adveka found herself navigating an emotional tightrope, balancing on the precipice between hope and the potential for heartbreak. The hospital room, with its stark walls and mechanical sounds, bore witness to the intricacies of human emotion, encapsulating the fragility of life and the resilience of love.

In the hushed stillness of the intensive care unit, where uncertainty and anticipation had gripped the air, a subtle shift occurred. The rhythmic beeping of the heart monitor persisted, but there was a change, a subtle cadence that hinted at the awakening of life. Yichen, who had been suspended in the silent depths of unconsciousness, began to stir.

Adveka, her eyes fixed on Yichen's face, saw the subtle signs of life returning. His eyelids fluttered, a gentle movement that shattered the stillness that had enveloped the hospital room. As awareness gradually returned, Yichen's eyes opened, revealing a momentary confusion that soon gave way to recognition.

The soft glow of relief illuminated Adveka's features as Yichen's gaze met hers. The hollowness that had lingered in the room began to dissipate, replaced by a tangible sense of renewal. Yichen's hand, once limp, now tightened its grasp around Adveka's, as if seeking reassurance in the midst of the disorienting journey between unconsciousness and awakening.

Their eyes held a depth of understanding that transcended words. Adveka, who had stood vigil by Yichen's bedside, witnessed the return of vitality to the man she had come to care for in ways she hadn't fully acknowledged until the orchestrated accident. The hospital room, once a stage for uncertainty, now became a backdrop for the fragile beauty of a second chance at life.

Yichen's voice, though initially hoarse, broke the lingering silence. "Adveka," he whispered, the single word carrying a weight of gratitude and acknowledgment of the presence that had been a constant during his unconscious sojourn.

It was a word that held within it a recognition of the emotional tether that had formed between them.

Adveka, her heart swelling with a myriad of emotions, managed a soft smile. "You're back," she said, her voice a gentle echo in the room.

Yichen nodded, his eyes reflecting the gratitude that words couldn't fully convey. The hospital room, once a space marked by uncertainty and the potential for heartbreak, now bore witness to the fragile yet resilient nature of life and the unexpected twists of emotion.

The medical staff, alerted by the change in Yichen's condition, entered the room with a mix of professional efficiency and relief. As they conducted their examinations and assessments, Adveka remained by Yichen's side, a silent pillar of support.

As Yichen traversed the path of recovery, the hospital room metamorphosed into a haven for shared moments, awash with the subtle whispers of romance. Enveloped in the gentle radiance of muted lights, Yichen directed his gaze towards Adveka, his eyes mirroring a symphony of emotions.

Their conversations, once tethered to the language of business, now pirouetted on the edge of something more profound. The orchestrated accident had become a catalyst, unraveling layers of formality and revealing the vulnerabilities that had remained hidden. Yichen's gaze, once absorbed in the intricacies of business strategies, now sought solace in the sheer simplicity of Adveka's presence.

As they navigated the uncharted waters of their deepening connection, their discussions traversed a spectrum of topics–from the profound to the mundane. Yichen found himself baring his soul, sharing fears and aspirations, while Adveka confided her dreams and the intricacies of her journey. The hospital room, once a space tinged with uncertainty, evolved into a haven for the exchange of not just words but the silent language of shared glances and mutual understanding.

In those tender moments, Yichen and Adveka realized that their connection transcended the confines of the hospital room. The quotes of poets lingered as a poignant reminder that joy could be found in the simplicity of shared moments and the authentic warmth reflected in each other's eyes.

In the midst of their evolving connection, Yichen's capable assistant, driven by determination and resourcefulness, delved into the intricacies of the orchestrated accident. Late one evening, in Yichen's temporary office within the hospital premises, the air was charged with anticipation as they gathered to examine the pieces of evidence.

The room, dimly lit to create an atmosphere of secrecy, housed a collage of photographs, documents, and digital files meticulously organized by the assistant. Yichen, Adveka, and the assistant pored over the details, their expressions a mix of intensity and resolve.

"These images were captured from the surveillance cameras around the accident site," the assistant explained, pointing at a series of photographs spread across the table. "There's a pattern here, and it suggests a premeditated plan."

Adveka's eyes narrowed as she examined the images, her keen intellect piecing together the puzzle. Yichen, usually stoic, betrayed a flicker of anger as he absorbed the calculated nature of the attack. The evidence pointed towards a deliberate orchestration, challenging the initial assumption that it was a random incident.

The digital files revealed a trail of electronic communications, indicating a network of individuals involved in planning the fatal attack. The room echoed with the clatter of keys as the assistant navigated through encrypted messages, slowly unraveling the sinister plot.

Yichen's voice, a steely edge cutting through the tension, broke the silence. "This wasn't an accident. It was a targeted assault. But why?" he mused, his gaze fixed on the evidence before him.

Adveka, her mind racing, spoke up. "Perhaps someone saw you as a threat, Yichen. A calculated attempt to eliminate competition or disrupt your business dealings."

The assistant, having unearthed a particularly damning piece of evidence, interjected. "I've found financial transactions that trace back to individuals with questionable motives. It seems like a carefully funded operation."

As the trio delved deeper into the evidence, the gravity of the situation became undeniable. The orchestrated accident was not a random act of violence but a meticulously planned assault with far-reaching implications.

Yichen's gaze shifted from the evidence to Adveka, a shared understanding passing between them. The revelations brought with them a heightened sense of urgency - not just for justice but also to protect against future threats. The hospital room, once a cocoon of budding romance, now transformed into a command center where the battle against those who sought to harm Yichen and his endeavors took shape.

The revelation of the heinous plan behind Yichen's orchestrated accident sent shockwaves through the corridors of power, prompting swift and decisive action. However, in the wake of this storm, a new threat emerged–one that had Adveka squarely in its crosshairs.

Late one night, as Adveka left the hospital premises after a meeting with Yichen and his assistant, a shadowy figure lurked in the darkness. Unbeknownst to her, the assailant struck with ruthless efficiency, catching Adveka off guard. The air echoed with a brief struggle, and before anyone could intervene, Adveka was left heavily injured, her strength ebbing away as the assailant vanished into the night.

News of Adveka's attack reverberated through the hospital, jolting the sense of security that had enveloped the space. Yichen, still recovering from his own ordeal, was filled with a profound sense of anger and helplessness as he rushed to Adveka's side.

The hospital room, once a sanctuary of budding romance, transformed into a somber battlefield where the casualties were not just physical but emotional. Adveka's injuries painted a stark reality, a stark reminder of the dangers that lurked in the shadows of their intertwined lives.

As the medical team worked tirelessly to stabilize Adveka, Yichen, fueled by a mixture of fury and determination, took charge. The evidence from the previous investigation now served as a roadmap to uncover those responsible for this new assault. The hospital room, which had witnessed their shared moments, became a makeshift headquarters for an urgent quest for justice.

Yichen's assistant, undeterred by the escalation of danger, delved into the depths of the digital trail, determined to unmask the individuals behind Adveka's attack. Yichen, a tempest of conflicting emotions, wrestled with guilt over the vulnerability he felt for being unable to protect Adveka.

The revelation of a second attack intensified the narrative, as Yichen and Adveka faced not only external threats but also the emotional fallout of these traumatic events. The hospital room, now fraught with tension, became a space where resilience was tested, and the echoes of their shared experiences would forever be altered by the scars of adversity.

As Yichen's assistant delved into the labyrinth of digital trails once again, a chilling revelation emerged. The same nemesis that had orchestrated the attack against Yichen, the YB Group, was now unveiled as the malevolent force behind Adveka's assault. The tendrils of their ruthless ambition reached into the very fabric of Yichen and Adveka's lives, entwining them in a web of danger.

Yichen, his eyes ablaze with a newfound fury, faced the shocking reality that the enemy had not only targeted him but had now set their sights on Adveka. His resolve solidified into an unyielding determination to dismantle the forces that threatened the lives of those he held dear. The hospital room, once a refuge for shared moments, became the epicenter of Yichen's storm of vengeance.

Confronting his top executives at YB Group, Yichen's rage erupted like a tempest. He spared no mercy, demanding answers, accountability, and swift justice for the assault on Adveka. The conference room, where strategic decisions were usually made, now echoed with the thunderous force of Yichen's anger, reverberating through the corridors of power.

Meanwhile, Adveka's condition deteriorated, casting a pall of despair over the hospital room. The ventilator became a lifeline, its rhythmic hum a stark reminder of the fragility of life. Yichen, torn between the battle for justice and the fight to keep Adveka alive, found himself navigating the tumultuous waters of helplessness.

The hospital room, now a battleground of emotions, witnessed Yichen's desperate pleas for Adveka's recovery. Every beep of the monitor, every hushed conversation among the medical staff, bore the weight of uncertainty. Yichen, grappling with the dual challenges of vengeance and the fear of losing Adveka, found himself in a relentless tug-of-war between the forces that sought to tear them apart.

Amidst the chaos of emotions and the palpable tension that gripped the hospital room, Yichen sought refuge in a private conversation with his steadfast assistant. In the dimly lit corridor just outside Adveka's room, the air was heavy with the weight of their shared burdens.

"Protect her, protect the future queen of the empire we've built," Yichen's voice, though low, carried the weight of an unspoken plea. His eyes, a reflection of turmoil and vulnerability, met the unwavering gaze of his assistant.

The assistant, recognizing the gravity of the moment, nodded solemnly. "I'll do whatever it takes, Yichen. We'll dismantle YB Group, piece by piece, and ensure Adveka's safety."

Yichen's jaw tightened, his fingers clenching into fists. "They will pay for this. No stone unturned, no mercy given. I want their name obliterated from the business field, their legacy erased."

His assistant, well aware of Yichen's ruthless determination, affirmed, "Consider it done. We'll expose the darkest side of their operations, reveal the rot within their foundations, and ensure they crumble under the weight of their own malevolence."

In that corridor, a pact was forged, sealed not with words but with a shared understanding of the battles that lay ahead. Yichen, a man accustomed to wielding power, found himself in the unfamiliar terrain of vulnerability. The ventilator's soft hum in the background served as a haunting backdrop, a constant reminder of Adveka's fragile state.

Adveka lay connected to the ventilator, her form fragile against the clinical white of the hospital sheets. Yichen's gaze lingered on her, a mixture of love and helplessness clouding his eyes. The room, once a witness to shared laughter and budding romance, now bore witness to a man grappling with the fragility of life.

He reached out, gently brushing a strand of hair from Adveka's face, the tenderness in his touch juxtaposed against the harsh reality of the situation. The ventilator's soft hum underscored the gravity of the moment, emphasizing the thin line between life and the void that loomed just beyond.

A chair scraped softly against the floor as Yichen settled beside Adveka, his eyes never leaving her face. In the hushed stillness of the room, conflicting emotions played out like a poignant melody. The determination to protect, to wage war against those who had caused this pain, clashed with the agonizing truth that, for now, he could do nothing to shield her from harm.

As he clasped Adveka's hand, his thumb traced soothing circles against her knuckles. The silent language of touch became a lifeline, a connection that transcended the barriers of words. Yichen, the formidable business tycoon, found himself stripped bare of the armor he wore in the corporate world, revealing a vulnerability he had never known.

The room became a nexus of emotions – love, frustration, and an overwhelming sense of responsibility. Yichen's jaw tightened, his gaze unwavering, as if by sheer willpower, he could shield Adveka from the perils that lurked in the shadows. The ventilator's persistent rhythm punctuated the silence, a reminder that time, fragile and fleeting, hung suspended in the air.

As Yichen sat vigil by Adveka's side, the hospital room transformed into a sanctuary of silent prayers and unspoken vows. The narrative, poised on the precipice of uncertainty, holds the promise of exploring the depths of Yichen's determination and the internal conflicts that unfurl within the crucible of a hospital room where love and vulnerability converge.

In the dimly lit hospital room, the air thick with the sterile scent of antiseptic, Yichen's usual composure began to crumble. The harsh reality of Adveka's critical condition weighed heavily on him, stripping away the armor of stoicism that had defined him in the corporate world.

As Yichen clutched Adveka's hands, the delicate lifeline that tethered him to the woman he loved, the monitors continued their rhythmic dance of beeping, each sound a painful reminder of the fragility of life. He sank into the chair beside her bed, his shoulders hunched with the weight of despair.

Tears, unbidden and unchecked, welled up in Yichen's eyes. The once indomitable force, a titan in the business arena, now found himself laid bare before the vulnerability of human emotion. His fingers trembled as he gently caressed Adveka's hand, as if seeking solace in the warmth of her touch.

"God," Yichen's voice quivered with an intensity that echoed through the hushed room. His plea reverberated against the stark walls, a desperate entreaty that defied the usual calm authority of his words. "Please, don't take her away. I beg you, bring her back. I can't lose her. Not like this."

The beeping monitors seemed to intensify, a dissonant soundtrack to Yichen's breaking heart. He bowed his head, the strands of his disheveled hair falling to obscure the anguish etched across his face. The room, once witness to shared laughter and budding romance, transformed into a sacred space where a titan of industry found himself vulnerable.

Yichen's shoulders heaved with the weight of grief, each breath a painful acknowledgment of the looming possibility of loss. The hospital room, a microcosm of life's uncertainties, bore witness to a man who had faced the cutthroat world of business but now felt defenseless in the face of the unknown.

In the stifling hush of the hospital room, Yichen's desperate plea lingered like a haunting melody. The beeping monitors, once an indifferent symphony to the ebb and flow of life, now seemed to echo the rhythm of his breaking heart. His tears, like crystalline tributaries, traced a path down his cheeks, falling onto Adveka's hand as he clung to it with a fierce determination.

The room itself felt suspended in time, as if the walls bore witness to an unfolding tragedy that transcended the usual realms of human experience. Yichen, the stalwart captain of industry, was now stripped of his veneer of control. The once domineering protagonist grappled with a force beyond boardrooms and business strategies – the fundamental power to preserve life.

His gaze remained fixed on Adveka's face, as if willing her to respond, to defy the impending darkness that threatened to engulf her. The soft hum of the ventilator, once a reassuring background noise, now carried the weight of uncertainty, underscoring the fragility of the life it sustained.

The room, bathed in the muted glow of medical equipment, bore witness to Yichen's internal struggle. Each tremor in his voice, every tear that fell onto Adveka's hand, revealed a man who, for the first time, confronted the stark reality that there were forces even he couldn't command. The power dynamics of the corporate world crumbled in the face of a power that transcended titles and positions – the power to preserve or relinquish a precious life.

As Yichen's plea hung in the air, it seemed to mingle with the charged particles of raw emotion. The boundaries between the physical and metaphysical blurred, and for a fleeting moment, the room existed in a space beyond the confines of mortal understanding.

The monitors, with their unrelenting beeping, bore witness to a titan's vulnerability. Yichen's shoulders, once squared with confidence, now trembled under the weight of an unfamiliar helplessness. The plea, charged with the intensity of a man grappling with forces beyond his control, marked a pivotal moment – a turning point in the narrative where the indomitable Yichen was forced to confront the limits of his influence, both in the corridors of power and the delicate dance of life and death.

The hospital room, once shadowed by the ominous presence of the YB Group, now basked in the victorious glow of Yichen's dominance. As he entered, an air of triumphant authority surrounded him, and the beeping monitors seemed to echo a different cadence—a rhythm of conquest and finality.

Approaching Adveka's bedside with measured steps, Yichen's eyes, typically unyielding, softened only momentarily as he surveyed the unconscious form before him. "Adveka," he declared, his voice a commanding undertone, "we've accomplished it. YB Group is eradicated. Their influence, their malevolence—erased."

There was a pause, as if Yichen expected acknowledgment from the still figure lying motionless. Adveka, connected to the life-sustaining machines, remained silent, an inert witness to the triumph being proclaimed. Yichen's gaze, though filled with the glow of victory, betrayed an undercurrent of poignant longing.

"Mirab," he continued, the word rolling off his tongue with an air of authority, "has ascended to unprecedented heights. Your brilliance, your vision—it lives on, pulsating in the veins of Mirab's success. The world is witnessing the realization of your unparalleled foresight."

While articulating Mirab's triumph, Yichen's words exuded dominance, each syllable a testament to the indomitable force he represented. Yet, beneath the veneer of conquest, a poignant thread of sorrow weaved through his voice. His success, in its grandeur, felt hollow without the one who had breathed life into Mirab.

Taking Adveka's hand with a firm yet gentle grip, Yichen pressed forward, his voice unwavering. "I have avenged. I have triumphed. Look at Mirab's new zenith. Mirab demands your presence. I demand your presence!" The declaration echoed through the room, each word a resounding proclamation of his supremacy.

In the aftermath of his assertive words, a moment of hushed silence enveloped the room. Yichen, the undisputed titan of business, stood by Adveka's bedside, the air thick with the paradox of victory tinged with an unspoken ache. The narrative, poised on the edge of Yichen's commanding presence, invites exploration into the intricate dance between dominance and the vulnerability hidden within.

The hospital room, a battleground of life and recovery, held its breath as Yichen re-entered, his gaze fixed on Adveka. The air was charged with a palpable tension, a delicate balance between the clinical precision of medical expertise and the tender threads of emotional connection.

Adveka lay on the hospital bed, her eyes now open but still adjusting to the harsh light. Yichen moved closer, a silent guardian hovering on the periphery of her consciousness. Her fingers, having released their vice-like grip on his hand, traced an unconscious pattern on the sterile sheets as if seeking reassurance.

The lead doctor, a beacon of calm authority, approached Yichen. "Mr. Yichen, she has been murmuring your name. It appears she's trying to communicate with you," the doctor explained, gesturing toward Adveka with a subtle nod.

Yichen nodded in acknowledgment, his eyes never leaving Adveka's face. The medical team, having completed their immediate interventions, discreetly withdrew, leaving the room bathed in the soft glow of monitor screens and the hum of medical equipment.

Adveka's lips moved, forming silent words that hung in the air with a sense of urgency. Yichen leaned in, his gaze unwavering, as if by sheer will he could decipher the unspoken language of her awakening. The room seemed to contract, focusing entirely on this delicate exchange between two souls intricately bound by fate.

"Yichen," her voice, though weak, carried a profound resonance. The name escaped her lips like a whispered plea, a longing woven into its very syllables. Yichen's heart skipped a beat as he registered the significance of the moment.

With a gentle touch, Yichen took Adveka's hand in his, grounding her in the present. "Adveka, I'm here," he reassured, his voice a soothing undercurrent in the room. The fragility of the scene contrasted with the steely determination that defined their shared history.

"Yichen," Adveka uttered once more, her voice weaving a delicate tapestry of emotions–threads of relief, yearning, and a profound sense of connection. Her gaze, now clearer, sought the reassuring depths of Yichen's eyes. In the gentle cadence of his name, she discovered a lifeline amidst the disorienting waves of waking up.

Yichen, the unyielding force, leaned in with a tenderness that belied his usual dominance. "Adveka," he responded, his voice a resonant echo of shared experiences. The room itself seemed to respond, reverberating with the resonance of their intertwined destinies–an intricate narrative that transcended the confines of corporate conquests and personal vulnerabilities.

As Adveka's consciousness settled, she began to articulate her thoughts. Her words, initially scattered fragments, gradually wove into a cohesive narrative. Yichen, perceptive to the subtleties of her expression, listened with a patience that mirrored the profound depth of their connection.

Their conversation unfolded as a nuanced dance, each word and silence a step in the intricate choreography of shared understanding. Adveka, with the finesse of a poet, unraveled the layers of her experience–the lingering echoes of pain, the unwavering resilience that had carried her through, and the undeniable bond that had endured the storms.

In this sacred exchange, the hospital room underwent a metamorphosis, transforming into a sanctuary of communion. Yichen, typically the indomitable business tycoon, seamlessly assumed the role of an empathetic listener. His eyes, fixed on Adveka's face, held a silent promise of steadfast support, decoding the unspoken language of her journey.

Together, they traversed the uncharted terrain of the present moment. The conversation, marked by pauses and reflections, became a vessel for shared truths and unfiltered emotions. The hospital room, once a stage for battles and recoveries, evolved into a haven where two souls reconnected, each word and silence weaving a tapestry of healing and hope.

As the dialogue continued, Yichen's unseen emotions wove into the fabric of their shared understanding. His feelings, often concealed beneath the armor of corporate stoicism, surfaced like unfelt threads in the intricate tapestry of their connection.

The soft hum of medical equipment created a gentle backdrop in the hospital room as Adveka's recovery continued. Gradually, the shadows of vulnerability that had clung to her began to dissipate, replaced by the returning glow of vitality.

As Adveka opened her eyes, the sterile hospital environment gave way to a welcome clarity. The room, bathed in muted light, held a serene atmosphere. Her gaze, shifting with cautious curiosity, scanned the surroundings until it settled on the figure by her bedside.

There, with a silent presence that spoke volumes, stood Yichen. His usually composed demeanor softened in the quietude of the moment. The lines of concern etched on his face bore witness to the battles they had faced together–the triumphs and the vulnerabilities that had unfolded in the intricate dance of their lives.

Adveka's lips curved into a grateful smile, and the air seemed to lighten as their eyes met. Yichen, the indomitable force that had stood by her side through storms, appeared more than just a business tycoon. In that moment, he was the anchor that had weathered the tempests of uncertainty.

"Yichen," Adveka whispered, the syllables carrying a blend of appreciation and affection. His name, spoken in the quiet space of the hospital room, felt like a familiar melody—a reassurance that resonated with the unspoken understanding they shared.

Yichen's eyes, a reflection of relief and genuine care, met hers. There was no need for elaborate words in that instant; the silent language between them conveyed more than any spoken language ever could. As Adveka extended her hand, Yichen clasped it with a warmth that transcended the physical touch.

In that serene hospital room, amidst the beeping monitors and the scent of antiseptic, Adveka and Yichen shared a moment of quiet celebration. It was a celebration of recovery, of enduring friendship, and perhaps, the acknowledgment of feelings that lingered beneath the surface—an acknowledgment that remained unspoken but deeply felt.

As Adveka settled into the rhythm of recovery, she found solace in the presence of the man who had been her unwavering support. The hospital room, once a space of uncertainty, transformed into a haven where healing and connection flourished.

After months of the sterile confines of the hospital room, Adveka finally stepped into the open air. The warmth of the sun on her face felt like a long-awaited caress, and the gentle breeze whispered promises of newfound freedom.

The world outside, vibrant and alive, welcomed her back with open arms.

As Adveka stood on the threshold, the soft hues of the sky painted a canvas of hope. The fragrant blossoms in the hospital garden beckoned her forward. With each step, the familiar scent of flowers mingled with the invigorating aroma of fresh air, creating a symphony of scents that marked her reentry into the world.

Yichen, attuned to the significance of this moment, stood a few steps away, allowing Adveka to absorb the beauty of the scene. His gaze, filled with a quiet understanding, mirrored the tenderness of the day. As Adveka closed her eyes, basking in the sun's embrace, a subtle smile graced her lips.

Unable to contain the overwhelming emotions that surged within her, Adveka turned towards Yichen. The distance between them closed in an instant as she walked into his waiting arms. The warmth of the sun seemed to pale in comparison to the comforting embrace she found there.

As Yichen wrapped his arms around her, Adveka felt a gentle release of emotions. Tears, like long-pent rivers, rolled down her cheeks. These were not tears of sorrow but of triumph, of overcoming the challenges that had tested her resilience. Each tear was a testament to the strength that had carried her through the darkest nights.

The embrace, bathed in the soft glow of the sun, spoke of a connection that surpassed the spoken word. It was a language of shared battles and triumphant reunions, a silent conversation that unfolded in the embrace of newfound freedom. Adveka, still teary-eyed, rested her head against Yichen's shoulder, finding solace in the familiar heartbeat that echoed the rhythm of their intertwined lives.

In that romantic moment, under the open sky, Adveka and Yichen stood as witnesses to the beauty of resilience and the profound tenderness that blossomed in the wake of challenges. The hospital garden, adorned with vibrant blooms, became a haven for their shared triumph over adversity.

The soft hues of the setting sun cast a warm glow on the scene, creating an ethereal backdrop for the emotions that unfolded. Adveka, her eyes reflecting the hues of the evening sky, turned to Yichen with a heart full of gratitude. The tears that glistened like pearls on her cheeks were not just remnants of the past but also the promise of a future painted with the hues of love and unwavering support.

Yichen, his gaze a mirror to the depth of their shared experiences, gently wiped away Adveka's tears. The touch, tender and reassuring, spoke of a connection that had weathered storms and emerged stronger. The gentle rustle of leaves overhead and the fragrance of blossoms in the air became witnesses to the silent vows exchanged between them.

In that tranquil moment, the world seemed to fade away, leaving only Adveka and Yichen in the embrace of nature's serenity. The garden, once a sanctuary of healing, now became a symbol of their shared journey—a testament to the beauty that could bloom from the seeds of adversity.

As the sun dipped below the horizon, casting a warm glow on the horizon, Adveka and Yichen lingered in each other's arms. The promise of a future, painted with the hues of love and unwavering support, hung in the air like a delicate tapestry. The tears, though born of challenges, became pearls that adorned the story of their resilience—a story that continued to unfold under the canvas of the open sky, illuminated by the tender glow of a promising night.

The tears, glistening like pearls in the sunlight, were not just tears of the past but also the promise of a future painted with the hues of love and unwavering support.

The evening unfolded in a quiet ambiance, with the soft glow of candlelight casting a warm glow over the dining table set for two. Adveka and Yichen, having weathered the storms of adversity, found solace in the simple joy of sharing a meal.

The aroma of a delicately prepared dinner filled the air, mingling with the rich scent of fresh flowers adorning the table. Adveka, wearing a gentle smile that mirrored the newfound tranquility within, sat across from Yichen. The flickering candlelight danced in her eyes as she looked at him with a depth that words could not capture.

Yichen, attentive to every nuance, poured a glass of wine with a graceful gesture. The clink of crystal against crystal echoed in the room, a silent toast to resilience and the victories they had celebrated together. The table, adorned with the finest china, spoke of an intimate setting crafted for a moment like this–one where the weight of the past was replaced by the promise of a shared future.

As they began to savor the carefully prepared dishes, the atmosphere was filled with a symphony of shared laughter and unspoken understanding. Adveka's fingers traced patterns on the tablecloth, a gesture that spoke of the quiet appreciation for the present moment. Yichen, ever observant, caught every fleeting expression that crossed her face, each telling a story of battles fought and triumphs savored.

Amidst the culinary delights, the clinking of cutlery, and the dance of candlelight, Adveka and Yichen found a language of love that transcended the complexities of spoken words. The meal became a celebration–a feast not just for the palate but for the heart, a culmination of their shared journey back to life after facing the adversities.

The tender exchanges, the shared smiles, and the moments of silence held a sweetness that lingered in the air. In the soft glow of the evening, Adveka and Yichen discovered that the simple act of sharing a meal became a sacred ritual–a testament to the bond that had withstood the trials of life.

As the night unfolded, they lingered at the table, savoring the last bites and the lingering moments of togetherness. The warmth of their connection, like a fine wine, only deepened with time, promising a future where each shared meal would be a reminder of the love and resilience that had transformed their lives.

As the evening wore on, the atmosphere between Adveka and Yichen became infused with a playful yet intimate energy. The remnants of their shared meal lingered on the table, and a comfortable warmth enveloped them in the soft glow of candlelight.

Yichen, his eyes reflecting a mischievous glint, leaned back in his chair with a satisfied smile. Adveka, her own gaze filled with a mixture of amusement and curiosity, looked at him as he reached across the table to take her hand.

"Adveka," Yichen began, his tone adopting a more playful cadence, "do you know what I've realized tonight?"

Adveka, intrigued, raised an eyebrow. "Tell me, Yichen."

A subtle smirk played on Yichen's lips as he replied, "I've come to the undeniable conclusion that you, my dear, are not just an extraordinary woman. No, you're more than that. You're my queen."

Adveka, caught off guard, chuckled at his theatrics. "Your queen, you say? And what does that make you, the king of charm?"

Yichen's laughter resonated in the room. "Well, if the crown fits," he teased, bringing her hand to his lips for a playful kiss.

Adveka, with a twinkle in her eye, feigned a regal air. "I suppose every queen needs a charming king by her side."

Yichen's gaze locked onto hers, his expression turning more earnest. "In all seriousness, Adveka, you've been the guiding light through the storms. My queen, not by title, but by the undeniable strength and grace you possess."

Adveka's playful demeanor softened into a genuine smile. "And you, my charming king, have been my anchor. Together, we've conquered more than our fair share of battles."

Their hands remained entwined on the table, a silent acknowledgment of the unspoken bond they shared. The playful banter had seamlessly transitioned into a moment of heartfelt connection, where the titles they playfully bestowed upon each other carried a depth that went beyond words.

In the intimate glow of the evening, Yichen and Adveka reveled in the dance of their shared laughter, playful flirtation, and the silent understanding that painted the canvas of their evolving connection. The unspoken promise of a shared kingdom, built on love and resilience, hung in the air like a fragrant whisper, inviting them to continue their journey together.

As the romantic banter lingered in the air, a subtle tension began to weave its way between Adveka and Yichen. The remnants of their shared meal lingered on the table, forgotten in the magnetic pull that seemed to draw them closer.

Yichen, his eyes filled with a mixture of desire and tenderness, leaned in slightly, his hand still cradling Adveka's. The room seemed to shrink, leaving only the two of them in a cocoon of shared moments. Adveka, feeling the subtle shift in the atmosphere, met his gaze with a mirrored intensity.

Their fingers interlaced a silent promise echoing between them. The playful banter from earlier had dissolved into a charged undercurrent of unspoken longing. Yichen's thumb traced gentle circles on Adveka's hand, a gesture that spoke volumes in the hushed intimacy of the moment.

Adveka's breath caught, her pulse quickening as Yichen's proximity became electrifying. The air hummed with anticipation, and the unspoken question lingered between them like an irresistible force. In that suspended moment, the world outside seemed to fade away, leaving only the undeniable pull drawing them closer.

Yichen's gaze dipped to Adveka's lips, a silent invitation that spoke of a longing that mirrored her own. The tension between them intensified, the chemistry palpable. A single heartbeat seemed to stretch into eternity as they teetered on the edge of a kiss, the promise of shared passion hanging in the air like a delicate thread.

The charged atmosphere, filled with unspoken desires, held a magnetic pull that neither could ignore.

Adveka's gaze, once playful, now bore a smoldering intensity. The laughter that had echoed through the room was replaced by a silence pregnant with anticipation. Yichen, equally attuned to the shifting dynamics, felt a surge of electricity in the air.

Their hands, still entwined, tightened in a subtle yet deliberate manner. The unspoken words hung between them, each heartbeat echoing the unexplored depths of their connection. The flickering candlelight cast shadows on their faces, accentuating the vulnerability that lurked beneath the surface.

Adveka's lips curved into a seductive smile, and Yichen's eyes held a promise that ignited the spark of chemistry between them. The playful banter had given way to a charged moment, where the air crackled with an intoxicating blend of desire and restraint.

In the pregnant pause, the tension swirled around them like a tempest waiting to be unleashed. The unspoken question lingered, daring them to bridge the gap between playful banter and the uncharted territories of passion. It was a moment suspended in time, where the chemistry between Adveka and Yichen simmered, threatening to erupt into a cascade of unbridled emotions.

As they locked eyes, the unspoken tension between them seemed to crescendo, reaching a point where the only way forward was to surrender to the magnetic pull drawing them closer. The room, once filled with laughter and playful banter, now held the promise of a different kind of intimacy—one that awaited exploration in the charged space between them.

Adveka sat in front of her dressing room mirror, the soft glow of vanity lights casting a warm ambiance around her. The room was filled with the fragrance of success, and she could hear the distant hum of excitement from the venue where Yichen's success party was about to unfold.

As she carefully applied the finishing touches to her makeup, her reflection in the mirror seemed to hold a myriad of emotions. The glittering gown she wore sparkled in the dim light, yet her eyes told a story of resilience and inner strength.

Taking a deep breath, Adveka seemed to summon the courage to vocalize the myriad of emotions swirling within her heart. "Adveka," she whispered to herself, her voice a melodic cadence in the stillness of the room, "look at how far you've come. From the ashes of rejection and the shards of a broken heart, you've risen, not as a victim, but as a survivor and, dare I say, a queen in your own right."

Her fingers gently traced the delicate lines of her necklace, each piece an emblem of the triumphs and tribulations that adorned her tumultuous journey. "Love," she murmured, as if the very word held a weight that transcended its letters, "you've sought it, the kind that fills your heart with warmth and understanding. And maybe, just maybe, you've found it in the most unexpected corners of life."

Adveka's gaze shifted to a picture on the dressing table – a captured moment from the journey she had undertaken. "You sought love, the kind that fills your heart with warmth and understanding. And maybe, just maybe, you've found it in the most unexpected of places."

A smile tugged at the corners of her lips as thoughts of Yichen flooded her mind. "Yichen," she mused, her eyes reflecting a mix of gratitude and admiration, "the king who came into my life when I least expected it. He's not just a success story; he's the embodiment of strength, charm, and the love your heart has craved for."

The room echoed with the distant sounds of celebration, but Adveka continued her soliloquy, a form of self-reflection that was both therapeutic and revelatory. "Tonight," she said with a quiet determination, "I step into the spotlight not merely as a successful entrepreneur but as a woman who has faced her fears, embraced vulnerability, and found love in the most unexpected corners of life."

A tender smile graced her lips as thoughts of Yichen inundated her consciousness. "Yichen," she continued, her voice now a soft melody, "with every beat of my heart, I feel the depth of our connection.

Tonight's success party isn't just about celebrating Yichen's achievements; it's a celebration of the journey – the highs and lows, the moments of self-discovery, and the unwavering spirit that brought me to this very moment."

Adveka stood up, the elegant gown flowing gracefully around her, as if echoing the newfound confidence that enveloped her being. "This celebration isn't just about Yichen's success; it's about the triumph of love over the trials of the heart. With Yichen by my side, I feel like the queen who has found her rightful king, and tonight, we revel in the magic that is us."

As she prepared to leave her dressing room, Adveka cast one last glance at the mirror. The reflection staring back at her held a sense of fulfillment, a testament to the strength she had discovered within herself and the unwavering love she had found in Yichen. With a heart full of gratitude and anticipation, she stepped into the night, ready to celebrate not only Yichen's success but also the enduring power of love that had transformed her journey.

The grand success party for Yichen was in full swing, with the venue adorned in opulence and a palpable sense of celebration. Adveka, dressed in a resplendent gown that echoed sophistication, descended the staircase with a grace that turned heads. Her attire, meticulously chosen and tailored, accentuated her elegance.

At the foot of the staircase, Yichen awaited her, resplendent in a well-tailored suit that bespoke authority and charisma. As their eyes met, a shared spark ignited, a silent recognition of the journey they had traveled together. The room seemed to dim, focusing its collective gaze on the couple that embodied success, resilience, and the power of love.

Adveka approached Yichen with a confident stride, her gown trailing behind her like a cascade of stardust. Her eyes, adorned with a smoky hue that matched the allure of the night, held a magnetic allure. What caught the attention of onlookers, however, was the bespoke jewelry she wore – a special creation, meticulously designed by her own hands.

The jewelry, a unique set crafted with precision and love, adorned Adveka with an air of exclusivity. The necklace, earrings, and bracelet complemented her attire seamlessly, each piece a testament to her creative prowess. Yichen, observing her with a mixture of admiration and pride, couldn't help but marvel at the intricate details that reflected their shared journey.

As Adveka and Yichen stood side by side, the spotlight of the party naturally gravitated towards them. The murmurs of awe and appreciation rippled through the crowd as they became the visual epitome of success and unity. The couple, twined in the artistry of their attire, created a tableau that encapsulated the essence of the night.

Their fingers intertwined as they shared a private moment amidst the public spectacle. Adveka, with a soft smile, conveyed a message that transcended words – a gratitude for the unwavering support and love they had found in each other. Yichen, his eyes reflecting a sense of fulfillment, reciprocated the sentiment, understanding the significance of this shared accomplishment.

Together, they gracefully navigated the crowd, their synchronized steps echoing the harmonious rhythm of their connection. The success party, designed to celebrate Yichen's achievements, now transformed into a celebration of partnership, love, and the intertwining destinies of Adveka and Yichen.

As they moved through the party, the unique jewelry Adveka wore became a symbol not just of artistic brilliance but also of a love story written in the details. The whispers of admiration followed them like a gentle melody, and in the heart of the festivities, Adveka and Yichen, united in their triumphs, continued to dance through the night - a testament to the enduring magic of their journey together.

The ballroom, adorned in elegance and bathed in the soft glow of crystal chandeliers, became the enchanting backdrop for Adveka and Yichen's dance. As the melodious strains of a timeless waltz filled the air, they found themselves drawn to the center of the room, where the dance floor awaited.

Adveka's hand gracefully rested in Yichen's, their fingers interlaced in a silent promise that transcended the rhythm of the music. The bespoke jewelry she wore glimmered under the lights, catching the reflections of the surrounding opulence. Yichen, in his tailored suit, held her with a gentle strength that mirrored the unwavering support he had provided on their journey.

The dance began, and the couple moved with a seamless harmony, twirling and swaying to the music. Adveka's gown billowed around her like a cascade of moonlit silk, and Yichen's confident steps guided them through the enchanting choreography of the waltz. The room seemed to disappear as they lost themselves in the embrace of the dance.

Whispers of admiration followed their every move, for the couple exuded a magnetic presence that captivated the onlookers. It wasn't just the refined steps of the dance that held their attention but the shared glances, the unspoken conversations exchanged through the language of movement. Each turn and dip spoke volumes of the profound connection they shared.

As they twirled beneath the shimmering chandeliers, a collective hush settled over the room. Adveka's laughter, a melody that echoed with joy, blended seamlessly with the music. Yichen, with a soft smile, guided her through the intricate patterns of the dance, a silent affirmation of the partnership they had forged.

In the midst of the swirling dance, Adveka and Yichen's eyes met - an exchange that conveyed a myriad of emotions. Gratitude for the journey they had conquered, love that had blossomed against all odds, and a shared understanding that they were not just dancing at a ball but orchestrating the symphony of their intertwined destinies.

The waltz reached its crescendo, and as the final notes lingered in the air, Adveka and Yichen came to a graceful halt. The applause that erupted from the attendees was a testament to the enchanting spectacle they had just witnessed. The couple, momentarily suspended in the center of the dance floor, shared a private smile that spoke of triumph and the shared joy of the moment.

As the applause continued, Adveka and Yichen, hand in hand, gracefully exited the dance floor. The ballroom, now alive with the melodies of celebration, embraced the couple whose journey had become a living testament to the magic of love and success. In each step, in each twirl, they had not just danced at a ball – they had danced through the pages of their own fairy tale, leaving behind a story of resilience, unity, and the enduring power of a love that had weathered all storms.

A week latter, as the sun dipped below the horizon, casting a warm palette of colors across the evening sky. Yichen, with an air of quiet confidence, led Adveka to a secluded garden bathed in the soft glow of strategically placed lanterns. The air was imbued with the delicate fragrance of blooming flowers, creating an enchanting atmosphere for what was about to unfold.

As they strolled through the garden, Yichen's hand cradling Adveka's, the ethereal beauty of the surroundings seemed to mirror the moment that hung in the air. A subtle breeze rustled through the leaves, creating a gentle melody that accompanied the hushed anticipation.

A quaint gazebo adorned with fairy lights emerged, standing at the heart of the garden. Yichen led Adveka towards it, a knowing smile playing on his lips. The gazebo, draped in cascading vines and soft fabric, exuded an aura of romance that promised something extraordinary.

As they stepped into the heart of the gazebo, Yichen turned to face Adveka, his eyes holding an intensity that bespoke a depth of emotion. He reached into his pocket, retrieving a small velvet box, and presented it to her with a graceful flourish.

Adveka's eyes widened in surprise as she took the box in her hands. The velvet felt smooth against her fingertips, and when she opened it, a gasp escaped her lips. Nestled within was a ring - not just any ring, but a testament to Yichen's elegance and uniqueness.

The ring itself was a work of art, a symphony of diamonds and sapphires intricately set in a design that spoke of timeless sophistication. The play of light within each gemstone created a dazzling display, casting a kaleidoscope of colors that danced in harmony.

Adveka looked up at Yichen, her eyes reflecting a mixture of shock, joy, and a growing realization of the significance of this moment. The garden around them seemed to hold its breath, as if nature itself paused to witness the union of two souls.

In a voice that resonated with a sincerity only found in the depths of love, Yichen spoke. "Adveka, from the moment our paths intertwined, I knew that ours was a journey destined for greatness. Today, in this enchanted garden that bears witness to the beauty of our love, I ask you to join me in a lifetime of shared dreams, laughter, and triumphs."

He paused, allowing the weight of the moment to settle. "Will you marry me, and together, let us create a future as splendid and unique as the love that binds us?"

The garden, alive with the soft glow of lanterns and the fragrance of blossoms, seemed to hold its breath in anticipation. Adveka, her heart echoing with the magic of the moment, met Yichen's gaze. In that heartbeat, where time stood still, she found her answer - a radiant smile that spoke volumes, and a nod that echoed a resounding "yes."

As Yichen gently slipped the exquisite ring onto her finger, the garden erupted in applause - an echo of nature's approval of this tale of love, elegance, and a proposal that surpassed all expectations. The couple, now engaged, stood in the heart of the enchanted garden, surrounded by the splendor of their love story, ready to embark on a new chapter of shared dreams and everlasting joy.

In the quiet moments of life, when the noise of the world fades away, Adveka found solace in the reason that made her smile. It wasn't just the triumphs or the grandeur of success; it was the simple, genuine moments shared with Yichen. Their love had become the unwavering anchor in the ebb and flow of life.

Yichen's companionship had been the constant thread that wove through every hardship, turning challenges into opportunities for growth. Together, they navigated the complexities of the world, hand in hand, finding strength in unity and comfort in each other's embrace.

Their bond, like a beautifully imperfect tapestry, complemented the flaws they discovered in themselves. In the vulnerability of shared moments and the acceptance of imperfections, their love flourished. Adveka realized that it was this love, deep-rooted in her heart and mind, that brought a profound sense of fulfillment and completeness.

As they stood on the precipice of their shared future, Adveka understood that the journey had been about more than just conquering business empires or achieving milestones. It was about building a life rich in love, understanding, and shared dreams. Yichen, the king of her heart, had been the orchestrator of this love story, and in the intricacies of their connection, she found the true essence of happiness.

The story wasn't just about the grand successes or the fairy-tale moments; it was about the quiet, everyday joys of knowing that someone stood by her side, understanding her in ways words could never capture. As they looked ahead, hand in hand, the love that had weathered storms and celebrated victories whispered promises of more adventures, more shared laughter, and a lifetime of enduring love.

In the tapestry of their lives, Adveka and Yichen had found the reason to smile, the companion to make every hardship fine, and the bond that beautifully complemented their flaws. This, Adveka knew, was the love that she would keep deep in her mind, a cherished melody in the symphony of their shared existence. And so, their story continued, an ode to love's enduring power, and a testament to the richness of a life well-lived together.